Praise for Errick Nunnally

"It's a 1970s coming-of-age story unlike anything I've read… a beautiful, elegant fantasy in a life where growing up Black in Boston is sometimes frightening and even dangerous, especially with the enemies his parents made a decade before."

—Christopher Golden, author of *Road of Bones*

"*The Queen of Saturn and the Prince in Exile* is a beautiful, messy, and profound coming of age novel, deftly exploring the joys and dangers of growing up Black in 1970s Boston. Part *The Brief and Wondrous Life of Oscar Wao*, *Fortress of Solitude*, and a comic book-style origin story, Errick Nunnally has penned a marvel. One that—in a fair universe—will put him on the radar of readers everywhere."

—Paul Tremblay, New York Times bestselling author of *Horror Movie* and *A Head Full of Ghosts*

"Gods, monsters, and comic books of 1970s America, and a family in the scope of the powers that be—I was instantly enthralled. Nunnally is a real talent."

—Laird Barron, author of *Not a Speck of Light*

"Errick Nunnally is a voice and storyteller you do not want to sleep on. This heartfelt novella gives you a deep experience of the otherworldly and the reality of being a black youth and man in America. Every moment of this book touched me in different ways, but I loved it all the same."

—V. Castro, author of *The Haunting of Alejandra* and *Goddess of Filth*

"Errick Nunnally has established himself as a powerful voice within the Afrofuturism canon and gifted us with an emotionally charged, uniquely American coming of age story. I can't recommend this book enough."

—Michelle Renee Lane, Bram Stoker Award-nominated author of *Invisible Chains*

"Drawn with wintry, coming-of-age affection, Errick Nunnally's *The Queen of Saturn and the Prince in Exile* is an intimate tale of personal sovereignty reclaimed and birthright restored. Here at the kitchen table, the love and deeply rooted energy of Black liberation is shared from mother to son. With this story at our fingertips and before the violences of our world, we are all invited as sojourners and witnesses to this realm."

–L. E. Daniels, Bram Stoker Award®
finalist, author of *Serpent's Wake: A Tale for the Bitten*

"Nunnally masterfully draws us into this mesmerizing coming of age story of a Black child whose mother tells him she's from another planet, while seamlessly folding in the struggle against discrimination. I couldn't stop reading as the mystery of his mother is unveiled at the same time as the horrific impact of racism wrecks their lives."

–Linda D. Addison, award-winning author, HWA Lifetime Achievement Award recipient, and SFPA Grand Master

"Endlessly inventive and blisteringly paced, Errick Nunnally's *The Queen of Saturn and the Prince in Exile* is like nothing else you'll read this year. A triumphant genre mashup with an unwavering undercurrent of heart, fans of the subversiveness of Victor LaValle and the ingenuity of David Wong/Jason Pargin will want to scoop this one right up."

—Christa Carmen, Bram Stoker Award-winning and Shirley Jackson Award-nominated author of *The Daughters of Block Island* and *Beneath The Poet's House*

THE QUEEN OF SATURN AND THE PRINCE IN EXILE

Copyright © 2025 by Errick Nunnally

All rights reserved.

Cover by Matthew Revert

ISBN: 9781960988621

CLASH Books

clashbooks.com

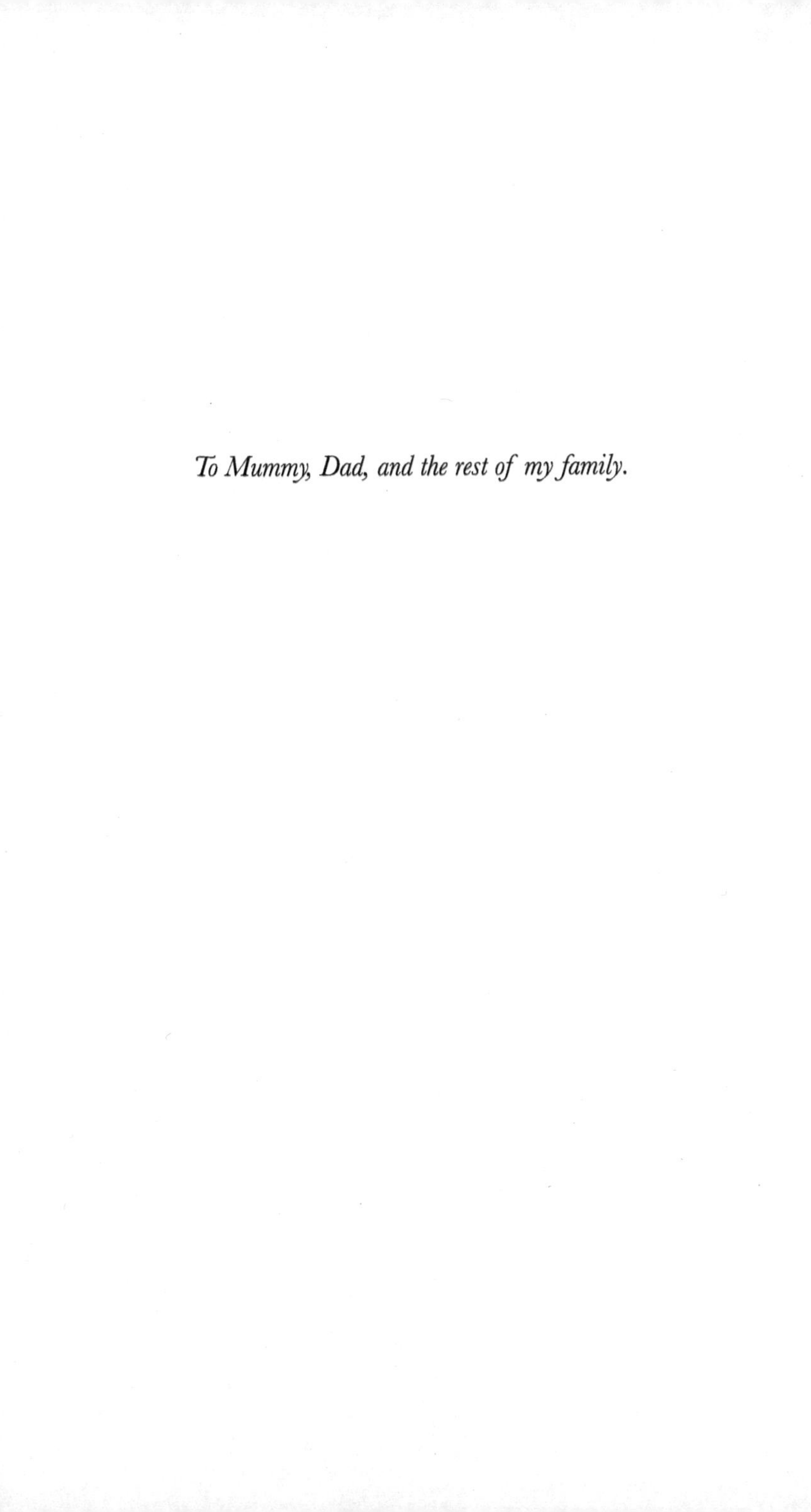

To Mummy, Dad, and the rest of my family.

Contents

THE QUEEN OF SATURN AND THE PRINCE IN EXILE

ERRICK NUNNALLY

Part One: The Ice Caves

———————————

The cold air scalded the inside of Sean's nose and he felt his eyelashes ice over with every blink.

DJ, the smallest, had shimmied through the basement window first, followed by Gerry, the tallest but slimmest, and now it was Sean's turn. He turned around, slid through the window, scooting backward while his rubber-booted feet dangled in space, and lowered himself to the ice-covered floor.

"Hurry up," Mike said. He was the latest addition to the group.

Sean was about the same size as the spectacled boy and knew his friend would have the same sort of trouble. It wasn't clear how DJ had managed, considering his shorter height. "I'm going as fast as I can, Peabody, gimme a second."

"Don't call me that, I hate it." Mike shoved his black-rimmed glasses back up his nose.

"Yeah, I know," Sean grunted and slipped all the way through the window, grateful when his toes brushed a solid surface. Standing on ice was an art. Especially wearing hand-me-down, faux-leather boots. The black, knee-high shoes were good at keeping snow out, but failed for traction and warmth. It paid to keep moving and he shuffled out of the way.

Mike slipped through even faster, after Sean's example.

Thick ice coated every surface in the basement. Rivulets of solid blue and white hung in a frozen cascade. The basement had been transformed into an ice cave, like something from a science-fiction movie. Only this was real. The triple-decker had burned three nights ago and temperatures had held well below freezing since then.

The tragedy happened all too often, when frigid temperatures settled in the region and space heaters ran all night. Like the news media, the boys hadn't given much thought to who had lived in the building, how their lives were upended and memories lost. Their only thoughts were on seeing how thousands of gallons of water, dumped on the building by the fire department, had settled.

"Wow," Sean said. Mike stood next to him.

"Yeah," Mike answered.

DJ slid into view, looking like a Muppet raised in the 'hood. Like all the boys, he wore multiple layers of mix-and-match hand-me-downs. His eyes were as round as they could be, above the scarf wrapped around his mouth.

"This is incredible!" DJ said.

From the other end of the basement, they heard a crash and the tinkle of broken ice.

"Hey, check this out," Gerry called. He'd found a thick column of ice that looked like a stalactite and stalagmite had met and grown to the width of an adult man. In both hands he held a pipe and took another whack at the column, showering the boys with shards of ice. In addition to being the tallest, Gerry was the oldest by two years, but his lack of progress in school put him in with the other three boys. Quiet, with an ever-deepening interest in music, he'd begun voraciously collecting records last year. He'd even bought the soundtrack to *Grease* and forced them all to listen to it—more than once—in a bid to convince them of the music's quality. Gerry had gone to the movie alone since none of them could bring themselves to watch Vinny Barbarino singing and dancing. That was the sort of thing white folks did, and it was embarrassing.

They scattered to explore.

Sean circumnavigated the basement, touching the ice as he went. It was bumpy, frozen in mid-flow, too thick to break easily. The floor was covered by at least six inches of ice that curved at the walls.

DJ slid by, almost choking on his obnoxious laugh, and Sean heard another crash of ice from Gerry.

Mike stumbled into view, his hard rubber soles barely finding purchase on the ice. "Find anything cool?"

Sean shrugged and said, "Just ice and more ice. I keep expecting Box to show up."

It was the kind of sci-fi detail joke that only Mike would pick up on. He grinned and snorted, moving past Sean to keep exploring. Gerry kept whacking at the ice column and DJ continued to slide back and forth.

Sean's mind wandered. The icy space reminded him of stories his mother, Sojourner, would tell him about her planet. The crystal caves her people had carved in Saturn's crust in order to survive beneath the gas giant's surface. She liked to remind him that she was over a thousand years old and an exiled queen. It was the sort of bright imaginings a mother who'd read comic books to her son came up with. The most fascinating thing about her stories was how consistent they were and that she clung to them without change. Sometimes he wondered—

A thunderous collapse of ice grabbed everyone's attention. Giant blocks of ice thumped loudly in the basement as Gerry's demolition project collapsed.

An eerie silence fell. Ice crystals floated through the basement and peppered their exposed skin with pinpricks of cold. For the briefest of moments, Sean's stomach contracted in fear that Gerry had been buried. He peeked around the corner and saw Gerry up against an icy wall. The tall boy had dropped his bludgeon and now stood with a look of unabashed surprise on his face. He started to giggle. It was infectious. Before long they all laughed at the unexpected moment.

"Hey, maybe we should keep it down," Sean said, through a final snort.

Movement outside the window caught his eye, startling him.

A shadow had passed in front of the window. In the next window, Sean saw a pair of legs dressed in blue pants and work boots. The figure squatted. A craggy, older man with puffy cheeks and a thick salt-and-pepper mustache peeked in. His girth and age prevented him from bending far enough to easily look in the window.

DJ had seen him too. "Oh, shit!"

Gerry sidled up to Sean and asked, "What?"

Sean said, "Someone's out there."

The man straightened and the boys watched his legs

take long strides to the rear of the building. For a moment, there was nothing but silence except for the occasional crack of ice, until a deep male voice shouted through the basement door, shattering their nerves. "Who the hell's fuckin' around in there?"

The basement door rattled. It remained closed, jammed by the thick layer of ice. The boys panicked and scrambled for the window they'd slipped in through.

DJ got up to the opening first and the boys pushed him out. Then Mike and Sean wiggled through. Gerry only had his head and shoulders out when they heard the shouting man coming around the corner.

They all looked, nearly frozen with fear, and Gerry made a strangled noise.

Sean shouted at DJ, "Help me!" They grabbed Gerry's arms and pulled him out of the window so fast that they were all able to stumble into motion, running away towards Norfolk Street.

The old man couldn't keep pace, but he swore long and hard at their backs. They pounded down the narrow trail of filthy, compressed snow on the sidewalk, rounded the corner, and ran as fast as they could, kicking up frozen rooster tails. In one block, they were in the park. There they stopped, panting and laughing. DJ flopped to the ground and rolled down a small hill leading to the playing field. Further along the berm, dozens of kids were sliding down the hill. Some had sleds, most were using pieces of cardboard, and one group of three had the hood of a car beneath them as they went screaming down the steepest hill.

"I wish we had a sled," Sean said to no one in particular, breath still coming in heaves.

"Yeah, me too," Gerry replied.

DJ was still at the bottom of the hill, squawking and likely soaked from all the snow he was tossing around.

Mike shook his head at the spectacle. "Let's go find something to slide with."

The boys agreed and called to DJ who was so self-involved with play that he didn't hear them.

Mike shouted, "Hey, Baby George, let's go!"

DJ stopped abruptly and surged to his feet, angry. They all knew he hated the nickname as much for his stature as his passing resemblance to Sherman Hemsley. The boy's light-skinned face, already red from the cold, seemed to get even redder.

"Pay attention, fool," Sean called. "We're going, come on!"

The rest of the day went like that, with the boys occasionally wanting and not receiving. What they did have was each other, for as long as that would last.

The blizzard came the following month. A huge storm that dropped several feet of snow. Its severity surprised everyone, stranding cars and grinding Boston to a stand-still. Nothing moved, no buses, no cars, no trucks. There was no sign of plows or tractors of any sort.

After two solid days of bone-numbing cold and wet, playing in the snow, and enjoying the unexpected time off, Sean found himself stuck inside while his cold-weather clothes slowly dried in the cool front hallway. He'd helped his father with shoveling as much as he could, but now he sat, arms and legs fatigued, resting with a cup of cocoa his mother had prepared. There wasn't much worse than pulling on wet clothes to go outside. Maybe tomorrow, or the day after he'd be able to go out again. The snow didn't appear to be going anywhere, anytime soon.

His room was a hodgepodge of past and present, toys of little interest strewn about with books and art materials. He thumbed through an *Avengers* comic for what seemed like the millionth time, every line of dialog, artwork, and advertisement committed to memory. In the hallway, one of the largest spaces in the apartment, his mother ran a rattling jigsaw, cutting a thick piece of wood into a puzzle. He supposed it was the last one he'd seen her working on, the closeup of the Hulk's face, drawn in Trimpe's style and painted in her own.

Beneath the heavy, metal desk in the corner—jetsam from his father's old offices—were the rest of Sean's comics in a cardboard box. He took the pile next to him over and swapped them for the oldest set. These were the comics his mother used to read to him when he was four and five years old. Flipping through the stack, it was mostly Kirby and Lee's early creations for Marvel. *The Mighty Thor* was the title his mother had read with the most gusto, but she'd especially enjoyed *The Incredible Hulk*, a simple-minded, but powerful being who wished only to be left alone. He reminded her of Frankenstein's monster. She also had a shine for The Thing of *Fantastic Four* fame. A man trapped in a rock-like body, struggling with the fact of his heroism in the face of his disfigured body. She'd once created an art piece out of clay affixed to a five-foot board by fashioning each rocky scale of The Thing's hide, and painting it accordingly. Sean thought it was magnificent, but it had no home in the increasingly crowded apartment, a fact Sean's father often pointed out. The piece was now moldering in the basement.

Bored, Sean wandered into the hallway where

Sojourner just finished the last cuts for the puzzle. It was all finishing touches from this point on. She pushed goggles up on her forehead and slipped work gloves off to pick at some of the rougher edges of the puzzle.

"Hello, my prince."

"Hi, Mom." Sojourner had called him her prince all his life. He was used to it. Others were not. As had become obvious when a camp counselor took a knee to read the opening lines of a postcard at summer camp.

"Help me clean up? I'll dust if you grab the broom."

Sean nodded and set to work with broom and dustpan. Sawing inside the apartment could get very messy if carried on for too long without pausing to clean up. The basement was too cold for woodwork at the moment, so that meant frequent breaks. Sojourner dusted the various sculptures, books, and knick-knacks on shelves lining the hall.

"Hey, Mom, you remember reading all those comics to me when I was a kid?"

Sean's mother had been the center of his life for all of his years. She'd always seemed impossibly long in both imagination and form. Long fingers and neck, a long smile on a thin face—like the one she flashed just now before answering.

"Of course I do. Why do you ask?"

"I was just looking at them."

"Hm," was all she said, in response. After dusting a few more shelves, she said, "They always reminded me of the people I grew up with. Fantastic, impossible, larger than life itself."

Sean nodded, he knew the story, she'd told it a hundred times.

"I never knew it though, it was always so normal to me, until we found Earth."

Sean asked, "What do you mean?"

Sojourner sighed and swiped up more sawdust. "That we were fantastic, but in different ways. Compared to humanity, I understood that. Disappointing in different ways too, but in one crucial way, the same." She'd stopped cleaning and stood fingering the pendant around her neck. It was a swirling gold, with diamond-cut facets surrounding a dull, muddy gemstone.

Sean swept and waited for her to go on.

"When change came, it was… unruly, violent. My family resisted change and it wasn't until I came here that I truly understood why the people did what they did. This place, this country, the struggle of people who look like… us."

Sean felt torn. Sojourner never told her story without a distinct edge of melancholy, of loss and wishful thinking. She'd never told the story this way, but the fine edge of disconsolate memories was still there. He worried about his mother. Her moods, the way she'd go still sometimes and stare into the air at things Sean felt he should be able to see, but couldn't.

Then Sojourner smiled. Clearly, a more positive thought crossed her mind. "It provided clarity for me, but not until after I'd met your father." She dumped sawdust into an empty coffee can and wiped her hands.

Sean grinned back, an awkward flash of emotion. He loved his father as well, for sure, but David Lenun spent most of his time working. It was only in the last few years, as Sean got older, that he grasped how important that work had been.

The reinforced door on the first floor boomed. Sojourner smiled again. Dad was coming in from the cold.

Part Two: A Strange Winter

David entered the apartment, still out of breath, to the smiling faces of his family: strange and beautiful Sojourner and the son she'd given him twelve years ago. In the midst of wriggling out of his coat, he stopped to snatch the watch cap off his head.

Sojourner strode over and placed both of her palms on David's cheeks and kissed him. Sean felt a burst of embarrassment and wondered why the feeling had come. His parents were nearly always affectionate. They sat close on the couch, slow-danced in the kitchen, and shared kisses coming and going.

"Hey, baby," David said, slipping his coat and boots off.

"You're sweating and freezing at the same time," Sojourner said. "Let me get some coffee going for you." With that, she headed down the hallway and into the kitchen.

Sean hugged his father. "Ew. Your back is wet! Did you get all the snow?"

David snorted. "Hardly. But we can get on the sidewalk and driveway now. Might've gotten further if you hadn't gassed out." He gave Sean a friendly nudge. "You good now?"

Sean rolled his eyes, chewing on a smile. He could still feel the hum of fatigue in his young muscles.

As if reading his son's mind, David put one long arm around his boy's shoulders and said, "I can see how tired you are, boy. You'll be fine tomorrow. I'm sure you'll be back out there, when your stuff's dry. If it's not dry in the morning, put your things on the radiator for a while." David looked at the mess of creativity in the hall. Sean knew it irked his father to see such disarray. "Huh. You helping your Mom clean up? Get that sawdust in the can. I'll pick up scraps."

They set about their tasks silently, plucking and sweeping. The only other sounds came from the kitchen as Sojourner got the percolating pot going. The sawdust can was almost full, Sean noted. His mother used the dust to create a sculpting paste for a kind of fresco effect on paintings. Scraps could become all sorts of things, like the art that hung on the walls.

David dropped wood bits into a box that Sojourner kept for miscellaneous use. Then he unplugged and wrapped up the power tools. When he finished, he stood and took in the house silently for a few moments. Sean watched him, curious.

"I ain't never been home this much before."

Sean shrugged. "We know you have to work."

"Indeed, I do," David said, not looking at his son. "That's one good thing this damn storm brought." He smiled at Sean. "A break."

Sean smiled back.

Sojourner walked back into the hallway and handed David a steaming mug.

"Seems like whenever I am here, I'm cleaning up after your mother."

Sojourner poked David and said, "Well, you're too early this time. I'm not done yet." She picked up a piece of fine-grit sandpaper and went to work on the edges of the puzzle she'd just cut.

"You don't think we got enough stuff cluttering up the house already?" As soon as the words left his mouth, David regretted sharing the thought. He knew where it would lead.

"You know I have to create, David, it's what keeps me sane on this planet."

David sighed. "I know, Soj."

"A thousand years," she said.

Sean smiled at the interaction. She was going to tell the story. Again. It probably annoyed his father, but Sean had grown up with it. The story was a familiar piece of lore for him, a comfort, something he shared with his mother.

Sojourner worked on the puzzle pieces. "I miss my people. We weren't always on Saturn, you know."

David, who'd been in the process of quietly backing out of the hallway stopped and made eye contact with Sean, creasing his eyebrows in confusion.

Sean returned a quick shrug.

Sojourner didn't catch her husband's retreat or skepticism, speaking like a woman hypnotized. "We left N'za-el Thom after the final war ended and the monarchy fell. The planet had been at the end of its life—we'd only accelerated the process—following the whims of royal edicts long passed. My father was deposed, but that didn't stop the cataclysm. Fortunately, we didn't need spaceships to leave, we had technology that allowed us to travel through space without needing to construct such clumsy things. Like tunnels of light, suited to our physiology."

Sean made mental notes, appending the stories she'd told of Saturn with this newer, seemingly older piece. He stumbled over the original planet's name. However, she'd uttered a string of consonants, hard and soft, around vowels pronounced in ways he'd never heard before. His mother hadn't spoken of this, of any time before Saturn. He'd always assumed that the ringed planet was the origin story. She stopped fiddling with the wood and instead fidgeted with the pendant around her neck.

"I was so young when we arrived on Saturn, the engineers were just carving massive caverns and passages in the planet's icy crust. An uneasy truce was born of necessity. Despite the end of hostilities, I was still a part of the royal family—the sole heiress, their de facto queen —and imprisoned for 'crimes of unreasoning' before I was old enough to commit them. They expected so much from me, from my gilded cage. The royals still had loyalists. They smuggled me out and sent me to Earth. I wonder if I've been gone long enough to satisfy them yet." She shrugged.

David raised his eyebrows, a look of confusion on his face. He realized his mouth was hanging open and his coffee had cooled. He snapped his lips together, kissed Sojourner on the cheek, and faded into the kitchen.

Sean said, "You think you'll go back, Mom?"

Sojourner smiled and leaned back. "Maybe. But not today." She winked at Sean.

The doorbell rang and David called from the

kitchen, "Who the hell could that be in seven feet of snow?"

———

Cold air filled the hallway and Sean could hear his father's voice echo up the stairs.

"Rome, you crazy muthah! Watchu doin' out in this frozen mess?"

For his entire life, Sean had known Rome, his father's best friend. He knew their friendship went further back than David's relationship with Sojourner. Sean waited by the door as the two men thumped up the stairs. He could hear the crinkle of plastic over their banter and movements.

To say that Rome was gaunt was to mistake him for weak. He looked like a pole of a man who'd be more comfortable on a basketball court than anywhere else, but the package camouflaged a fiercely intelligent person. He was a quintessential brother, a true believer in Black liberation, and an endless reader. It was such a part of him that it had become a part of his standard greeting. The word "revolution" was never far from his lips.

"Sean, m'little man, how goes the revolution?" Rome held a fist out to Sean.

"I still don't know what you mean by that," Sean said, bumping fists with Rome.

"Oh, you will, little brother, one day you will!" Rome's words seemed to come from his entire body, the way he turned his head, shook his shoulders, and leaned to emphasize his speech.

"Shoes," Sojourner said, without looking in Rome's direction.

"Oh, right. Sorry, Soj." Rome kicked off leather high-tops, revealing thick gray socks, and minced over to Sojourner to kiss her on the cheek. He kept his green jacket on, jamming gloves into the pockets.

She smiled and said, "Hello, Rome," but continued working on the puzzle.

Sean looked at Rome's shoes. The man had been wearing sneakers in this insane snow. It boggled Sean's mind.

David slapped Rome on the back and hugged him with one arm. "What's with all the bags, man?"

"Liberation, my brother. C'mon, in the kitchen."

Sean followed the men. Rome dumped the bags on the table. Steaks spilled out. Some packs of ham. Chicken pieces of all sorts too. All shrink wrapped over styrofoam plates with sticker prices and Star Market branding. Mixed amongst the meat were other things such as fresh vegetables, and boxed items like cereals and pasta.

"Whoa!" Sean marveled at the haul.

Rome and David ignored Sean's outburst and subsequent pawing through the pile.

Stunned, David said, "What is up with *all this*, Rome?"

"Yo, Dazzman, we snowed deep in here. You check the boob tube, see all them National Guard plowing white neighborhoods? And where we at? Still under seven feet of snow and runnin' low on supplies. Well, the market's right over the bridge. Look like the snow caved in one o' the big windows, so me an the brothers decided to become distributors." Rome smiled. And when he did, all the deep lines on his dark face curved and he showed all his teeth through a dense beard, between thick lips.

"My man!" David cranked his right hand far back

and Rome did the same. Their palms cracked together and they pulled each other close.

Sean looked up from the pile of meat to see his mother in the doorway, an unreadable expression on her face as she regarded the two men. When she noticed Sean looking at her, she nodded, a little curve at the corners of her mouth and went back to her project.

Sean wasn't sure what to think about this. Was it stealing? Would it get them in trouble, would anyone know? It was beyond imagination what might happen if he'd done something like this. He looked up at his father and Rome and said, "Are we gonna be able to fit all this in the fridge?"

The two men laughed.

"I'm sure we'll figure it out. Besides, there's a whole freezer outside, so we can always store some meat on the porch. How about you get started? Put the vegetables away."

"Okay." Sean set about moving the produce to the correct bins in the refrigerator. As carrots, celery, and some root he didn't recognize bonked around in the trays, a very random thought crossed his mind. "Hey, Rome?"

Rome turned towards Sean, spread his arms and leaned back. "Yo, Sean, what's happenin'?"

Always so extra, Sean thought. "You were there when my Mom and Dad met. How did it happen?"

"Oh, man, they met and fell in love. What got you thinkin' 'bout that, young blood?" Rome's entire face scrunched up and he shook his head from shoulder to shoulder like Stevie Wonder.

Sean grimaced. "That's... not much of an answer."

Rome looked to David who shrugged and said, "He asked *you*."

Part Three: Origins

Rome sighed and said, "Look here, little man, we was working for the revolution—"

"What does that mean?" Sean's tone was innocent, curious.

"We was members of the BDP, my brother, the Black Defense Program, your pops and me."

"Was that like the Black Panthers?" As much as the decor of the home reflected the Black power values that simmered during the 1960s, Sean knew precious few details about the movement.

Sojourner often made art that reflected the Black experience—like the blue pieces that were portraits of child soldiers from Idi Amin's army to young Black men in the Vietnam War. Mothers. Fertility. Kings and queens. Protest. And one that showed the Panthers in a long line wearing berets and dark glasses while holding rifles.

Rome shrugged. "Kind of. We was focused on the mind, enlightening brothers and sisters, organizing political power through education and such. Okay? Here. Sit down." They both took a seat at the table, its meat pile dwindling as David put packages away.

"There was a time, in this country, that the U.S. Government wanted nothing more than the eradication of the Black man."

"And woman," Sojourner called from the hall.

Rome winced. "*And* woman, sure."

"And indigenous," Sojourner added.

Rome sighed. "May as well add the liberation of Puerto Rico, Soj."

"May as well," she said.

"Slavery?" Sean asked.

"Much later than that—yo, Dazz, you not tell your boy 'bout all this already?"

David shook his head. "He's only just now old enough to understand. We're not in the middle of that anymore and… I just never found the time." Sean's father shook his head again.

Rome waved it off, turning his attention back to Sean. "You ever hear of COINTELPRO?"

"No."

Rome shot David a dissatisfied look. David ignored it.

"I guess I shouldn't be surprised. Look, the FBI ran a COunter INTELligence PROgram—get it?"

Sean nodded.

"—to disrupt and attack all sorts of folks they didn't think were American: Black folk, the red man, and everything in-between. They targeted the American Indian Movement, Puerto Rican independence groups, all sorts of civil rights organizations. Hell, I wouldn't be surprised to find out they'd been involved in King's assassination."

Sean was taken aback. He knew Black history had been rough, but not like this. As near as he could tell, the country was on the right track; things were progressing. Weren't they? He looked at his father. David wore a sad look on his face.

No. That wasn't right.

David looked tired, exasperated. Sean didn't understand the emotions his father was projecting. He listened for his mother's artistic puttering, but the apartment was silent.

Rome leaned back and sighed. "By the time they got to our organization, the program was officially on the ropes."

"COINTELPRO? How, what stopped them?"

Rome snickered. "A bunch o' true freedom-lovin' brothers broke into an FBI office lookin' to destroy draft cards. Muhammad Ali had all them pigs distracted—"

Sean's eyebrows shot up. "Muhammad Ali was part of it?"

Rome tossed a nasty look at David again. "Yo, man…"

David sighed. "I know. The boy's a reader, but he likes reading science fiction and stuff. He'll get there."

Rome hummed, a noncommittal sound, and continued with Sean. "The point is: these dudes broke in for another reason, but found all these records incriminating the FBI, detailing all their illegal bull. Now, check this out, the first thing they did was turn the evidence over to the press in order to expose the whole thing. Know what the press did?"

Sean shook his head.

"Nothing. They did nothing. 'Cause the *white* establishment is always complicit, you can't trust none of them."

"Rome…"

"You know I'm right, Dazz."

"You were right back then, you may be right *now*, but we don't know what the future holds just yet." David made a gesture towards Sean.

Rome and David locked eyes. Sean's attention darted from one man to the other. Then Rome smiled and shrugged.

"So how did my parents meet?" Sean asked.

Rome sighed. "Well… Like I said, we was at the tail end of that FBI program when they started lookin' into us. We had a protest and education rally going down-town—attendance was good. That's when the FBI bombed us—"

"What?" Sean exclaimed.

David said, "We don't know who set the bomb off—"

"—It was the FBI or some fascist group they was funding—"

"—We don't know that eith—"

"And they tried to blame us," Rome said.

"Well, that's one hundred percent true," David said, "But we don't know where the explosion came from."

"Was anyone hurt?" Sean asked.

"Your mother," Rome said, "a couple other people."

"What? Wait." Sean exclaimed again.

"Okay, okay, look here." David held his palms forward, arms out in surrender. "We didn't know your mom, at the time, but she was there. There was an explosion—"

"—A bombing—"

"—Fine. *A bombing.* Your mom was hurt, I was the

first one to see her. The cops had been swarming, arresting and hurting people. They were always looking for an excuse. It was chaos and the cops weren't helping, they wanted us gone. I grabbed your mom and Rome helped us escape in the confusion."

Sean was shocked and it showed. "Was Mom hurt bad?"

David took a deep breath and chewed the inside of his lip. "Your mom… she healed up quickly, no scarring afterward, so, I guess not bad, but—"

"That's when I arrived." Sojourner stood in the doorway. Everyone looked to her. "The lightyear tunnel had been rushed—or they didn't know how to properly operate it. No one intended for such a violent arrival. It was supposed to touch down somewhere more remote. I was still acclimating to this environment when I met your father." She smiled warmly in her husband's direction.

David stared at his wife with a humorous, skeptical look while Rome chuckled and said, "I guess that's why there was no evidence of an explosive."

Sean's father crossed the kitchen and kissed his wife. "*I guess* if the arrival'd been done correctly, we'd have never met."

Sojourner smiled again and slid one arm around her husband.

"A'ight, folks, I gotta Robin Hood out." Rome popped to his feet.

"But…" Sean said.

"Peace, my young learner, I'll see you later."

David and Rome embraced again, exchanging encouraging farewells. He kissed Sojourner on the cheek.

"But…" Sean said, again.

And Rome left.

The farther away he got, the louder Rome became. He and David exchanged jokes and farewells until the heavy door at the bottom of the stairs boomed shut. Sean stood in the hallway, a bit awkward, considering what to do until dinner. He was standing next to a small bookcase and he absentmindedly perused the titles. Dragging a finger along the spines, he stopped and pulled Alex Haley's *Roots: The Saga of An American Family* from the shelf. His father closed the door and chucked him on the shoulder. Sean knew his father had wanted him to read this particular book for some time now.

David retired to the living room and Sean heard the television pop to life. His mother had begun sketching something. A new project, no doubt.

"No one ever believes me," she said without looking up from her sketch, a smile playing at her lips.

"Not even Dad?"

Sojourner let out a small exhalation of air. "Oh, he knows better."

Sean fidgeted with the book for a moment before saying, "I… believe you."

At this, Sojourner looked up from her sketch, pencil poised above the pad. "I know you do, my prince."

Sean felt a small zing of embarrassment at the title his mother used so often to refer to him. He said, "But how did you get I.D. and stuff?" Then he remembered the laminated card in the top drawer of his dresser. "And social security and all that?"

Sojourner took a deep breath and said, "It was a very different time then. People who look like us were very much on the fringes of America's society. We had to make do for ourselves so often, that acquiring things like that wasn't as hard or uncommon as you might think. Times change, though." She pointed at the book in his hands. "Those times are far behind you, but important to remember."

Sean looked at the book in his hands. The cover was simply an orange-to-black gradient, no people. When there were people on the covers of books, they were never black, he'd noticed. This book was about a Black family and even it didn't have Black people on it. "What were your people doing when this was happening. Did they have slaves?"

Sojourner looked thoughtful for a moment. She answered, "My people never sold each other, but they did kill each other." Then she went back to sketching.

Spring found Boston shortly after Sean finished reading *Roots*. He wasn't sure what to think about it. Most of the story was sad or terrifying and very different from his own experiences. Alex Haley's family survived, he supposed, but in no way intact. As he put the book back on the shelf, he wondered what it'd be like to trace his own origins. Only his father's connections were known and Sean knew them all, or knew of them. Some relations were in New York or down south in Virginia. He'd never met them or, more truthfully, he'd met them when he was too young to remember. Still, more remote family remained a topic of conversation at barbecues and holiday meals.

His mother only spoke rarely about her family and when she did, it was tangled up in her tales of Saturn. When he'd asked his father, he conceded that he didn't know much but that Sojourner likely had a fraught relationship with her parents and such. Which basically meant that she didn't want to talk about it.

It was the weekend and the day was warming up nicely. He picked up the phone with the long cord in the hallway, but before he dialed, the off-the-hook tone stuttered. He pressed the spring-switch to hang up and listened again. More stuttering and soft clicks. He shrugged and dialed Gerry's number. After four rings, Gerry's mom picked up.

"Hello, this is Sean, may I speak to Gerry, please?"

"Oh, hi, Sean! How are you doing?"

Sean could hear the warmth in her voice and it was easy to picture her smile. Gerry's mother was the friendliest of all their moms, but Sean never quite knew how to talk to her. "I'm good, Mrs. Donham."

"Hang on, Gerry's lazy butt is in his room." She took the phone from her ear and shouted her son's name. Sean could hear her telling him who was on the phone.

"Yo," Gerry said, "what's up?"

"Nothing. You want to go outside, maybe play some ball?" Sean wasn't that big a fan of basketball, but the sport dominated the neighborhoods and, besides, he hadn't played since last fall and it was fun with friends.

"Sure. Lemme grab my ball. I'll call Mike, you call DJ."

"Cool. Let's meet at Norfolk Park."

Gerry groaned.

Sean grimaced. He'd forgotten that Gerry had some trouble with Woolson Street boys last summer at that park. "If you don't want to go up there, that's okay. Umm, we could go to the Roslindale gym."

"Ah, that's too far. It's fine. See ya."

"Later." Sean hung up and dialed DJ's number.

Afterward, he put on some shorts and grabbed a sweatshirt. "Mom!"

"Yes, my prince?"

Sean cringed. "I'm going to the park!"

"Come back before dinner."

"Okay, Mom." He opened the door. "Oh. Hey, Mom?"

"Yes? Come here, it's hard to talk this way."

Sean sighed and closed the door. He found his mother on the back porch, the back door open. That was the only reason they'd heard each other in the first place. She was painting large panels of wood in blue. Nearby, a small pile of black and white paintings on torn paper awaited her. Sean surveyed the mess, seeing the cans of decoupage and shellack amongst scrap wood, thin nails, and wire. She was assembling a mixed-media piece.

Sojourner glanced at her son and gestured at the stack of paintings. "What do you think?"

Sean had seen the paintings in-progress. Each of them was a young Black soldier from past wars.

"People who look like us have fought in just about every war, everywhere. Some as young as this boy, in Uganda." She plucked at the portrait of a child soldier.

The paintings were excellent. Thick shadows, depths of black, and unmistakable ethnic features. As cool as they were, Sean had no interest, his mind was focused on catching up with his friends.

"Uhm, these are great," he said. "I heard some weird noises on the phone, I think it might be broken or something."

"Hm." Sojourner started painting again. "Tell your father when you see him."

"Okay."

Sean ran through the house, down the stairs, and out

the door. It was the exact amount of time needed to forget what his mother had told him to do.

Sean stood with his friends on the sidelines. They had next. Gerry bounced a basketball as casually as he walked or spoke or did anything. DJ hopped from foot to foot, a stream of commentary falling from his lips as he observed the somewhat older boys currently playing on the court. Both Sean and Mike exchanged nervous glances, full of uncertain energy for the game.

Norfolk's court was split in two with unused, netless tennis courts taking up half the area. A high fence walled off the space for basketball. A serious bonus was that both hoops and backboards were intact, nets and all. Kids—mostly boys—stood along the edges, as close to the fences as possible. Sean wasn't sure he'd ever seen a girl play ball. If they were around, it was to double-dutch on the tennis court.

Everyone knew it was a serious breach of protocol to interfere in any way with a game in progress. On some courts, kids would shoot a few baskets while the action boiled at the other end. Those kids found out the hard way where and when that sort of behavior was tolerated. The other parts of the park were dominated by a run-down playground that Sean remembered spending time on when he was much younger. A boulder split entirely in half separated a neglected soccer field from the play-ground. He remembered the stone as something more imposing than it was in the present. The entire back of the park beyond the soccer field bordered train tracks that led to parts unknown.

The boys on the court played hard, charging up and

down the lines, breath coming in blasts. Trash talk was reserved until after feats of athleticism had been demonstrated. The two teams respected each other, but that wasn't always a broadly shared sentiment.

"Damn, only a two-point lead again. They ain't never gonna finish," DJ said.

Sean looked at DJ. "What?"

"Two points, Sean. Someone gotta win by more than two, so if the wrong team scores…"

"Right, got it." Despite basketball being the king of sports in the neighborhoods, Sean had only a working knowledge of the rules. The more esoteric rules of street-ball never stuck in his mind.

"C'mon, whatchu got, white boy?"

The comment brought Sean's attention back to the court. The press of bodies felt warm in the cool air. The grunted comment came from Peanut and he'd been talking to Dom. Sean knew the dark-skinned Peanut from around. They weren't friends, not even acquaintances. He knew *of him*, mostly, and the older boy worked hard on the court. Same as Dom. Dom was one of the lightest boys in the neighborhood, with thick, nearly blond hair. 'White boy' was how Peanut hassled Dom, and he was the only one who got away with it. If anyone else said it, they'd have to deal with both Dom *and* Peanut. The two needled each other incessantly.

Watching both of them, Sean felt intimidated by their athleticism, their general presence. It was a feeling he hated and struggled to keep a tight rein on. The fact of the matter was that they were all roughly the same size, but some of their personalities made them seem a foot taller.

"Ain't no white boys 'round here, doo-doo." Dom

pulled up for a jump shot that snapped through the net and into one of Peanut's teammate's hands.

DJ groaned loudly.

Without thinking, Sean said, "Used to be lots o' white folks around here."

Peanut said something to Dom and they both rolled their eyes, but Sean missed it.

A shot thumped off the boards and the boys came charging back down the court, sneakers grinding on asphalt as Peanut's team scrambled on defense. A quick pass to Dom sent him charging into the paint. Two defenders followed, but he no-look passed it and his team scored an easy two.

DJ shouted, "Game! Let's go, we're up!"

Peanut shook his head and tossed Dom a look.

Sean didn't think DJ should be so openly enthusiastic. As they took to the court, Gerry fell to the ground. Peanut had cut in front of him, letting one leg move slow enough to be an unseen obstacle.

"Ooh, sorry, bruh, that was my bag. You okay?" Peanut held out a hand to Gerry.

"Yeah," Gerry mumbled and reached for the offered hand.

"Psych!" Peanut jogged backward, to the sidelines, waving goodbye, leaving Gerry to haul himself off the asphalt.

Dom and his team let the boys warm up. As they passed the ball around, taking shots, and moving around their hoop, Sean could feel all eyes on them. If they won, they could hold the court. They weren't in any way a serious threat, however. More of a break in routine for the intense, regular players.

Sean sunk a shot banked off the board when he felt a

palm between his shoulder blades. He'd nearly backed into Dom.

"Yo, what was you saying about white people 'round here?"

Sean couldn't tell if the older boy was being confrontational or simply asking. "Just that this whole neighborhood was mostly white folks. Jews."

"How you know that?"

Dom seemed genuinely curious, this time. Sean felt tension leak from his chest. "My pops told me. When he moved here, there was lots of Jewish white folks. This was like a suburb of Boston. Then they moved even further away. South."

"Huh. Don't no kind o' white folks want to live among us negroes, I guess. Okay, well, y'all ready?"

Sean shrugged, "I guess."

Dom shouted, "Yo, is the Washington Generals ready to go?"

Onlookers laughed a bit too hard at that, Sean thought, but it was what it was. The game was on.

DJ yelled, "Check!"

When Mike passed DJ the ball, the smaller boy charged down the court, short legs pumping wildly.

Sean exchanged knowing looks with his teammates as DJ careened into the paint, leaped into the air, and bricked the ball off the backboard.

Dom's team came at them four strong as DJ bounced off the chain-link fence leaving three to fend off an organized offense. It took six more baskets like that to calm DJ down.

Regardless, the rest of the game wasn't much different anyway. Dom called out NBA players' names whenever he took a shot. More often than not, the ball went in the hole for him.

Gerry scored the most points for them. He could handle the ball and sank jump shots with some regularity. It was the only thing that delayed the inevitable. They stuck around after the loss, waiting to see if they could get next again, and chatting into the evening.

As street lights came on, Sean and any other boys under strict orders went home while the others played on.

The house was heavy with the smell of hot grease. Sean knew that his mother was frying pork chops and mashing potatoes. If she included peas, it was definitively one of Sean's favorite meals. The chops were thin and coated with spices, but in his cooking ignorance, the only spices he recognized were salt and pepper. He'd eat right through the fat and gnaw on the bones in between shoveling a particular balance of buttery potatoes and steamed peas into his mouth. It was the type of meal he couldn't get enough of and it always threatened to burst his belly on the rare nights Sojourner prepared it. (For days afterward, the kitchen stank of grease, so it wasn't anywhere near a weekly staple for the family.)

As he waited, Sean struggled through algebra homework, his frustration building after weeks of instruction. It didn't help that the previous day's humiliating losses on the court still nagged. It seemed as if the symbols meant nothing. The equations slid from the page as they slid from his memories. He worked in pencil, erasing every other scribble. A stack of scrap paper with increasingly urgent writing grew next to him. Frustration gave way to despair. He fidgeted uncontrollably, one leg wobbling left and right and making contact with the side of the metal desk. His chair, an industrial office castoff, creaked under his shifting weight. The constant thumping created a low hum in the room, the drumbeat of circular thought. Despair gave way to anger and Sean bore down on his pencil, making darker and darker marks. Something clicked in his mind, like pouring puzzle pieces from a box that all fell together. The world dropped away and he flew through the next three equations before he realized his father was standing in the doorway, calling his name.

"You can't hear me, boy? It's dinner time. Stop making all that noise and come eat."

Sean turned in his seat, shocked back to reality. When he met his father's eyes, David had a curious look on his face. "Sorry, Dad. I was—"

"Are you all right?" David stepped into the room and glanced at his son's homework.

"It's algebra. I hate it."

David put one hand on Sean's shoulder and said, "Looks like you were finally getting it, though."

"I guess so." Sean tapped his pencil on the paper. The last few problems were markedly different from the rest. "I'll go back and fix the rest after dinner."

David nodded, took one last curious look at his son, and exited the room. Sean followed.

At the table, after all plates were filled, Sean dug in as expected, thoroughly pleased with the chops. "So good, Mom," he said, around mouthfuls.

Sojourner smiled and made eye contact with David who shrugged and grinned.

"He's not wrong," David said.

She looked down at her plate. "I'm glad."

They ate in silence for a few more bites until David said, "Looks like Sean figured something out in algebra. You should see his worksheet, it's like you can see the moment he figured it out." David raised his brows, holding his eyes on Sojourner.

She spared him a glance and said, "I'll take a look later."

"Oh!" Sean said, putting his knife and fork down with a clatter. "I forgot to tell you, Dad. I was on the phone the other day and I heard some weird clicks and stuff and Mom said I should tell you 'cause it sounded like the line's messed up or something." He went back to eating.

David looked from his son to Sojourner and back, twice. Sojourner shrugged—something she rarely did— and David said to Sean, "You, uh, heard it again, since then?"

"Haven't used the phone," Sean said around a mouthful.

"Okay, okay, thanks. I'll check it out."

Sojourner finished her small plate and took it to the sink.

David mumbled, "Excuse me," and picked up the kitchen phone. He stepped into the dining room proper, trailing the long cord, listening. He heard nothing but a steady tone. He dialed Rome's number. From the kitchen, he heard Sean ask for another pork chop.

Rome picked up on the third ring and said, "Yo." It was how he always answered the phone.

"Hey, man, it's David."

"What is up, Dazzman, my brother?"

Rome's enthusiasm, after all their dizzying years together, still put a smile on David's face. He felt a pang of guilt for what he had to say next. "You still got my bean pot, right?"

David could hear Rome shift the phone to his other ear. "Yeah, man, I still got it."

"Can you meet me tomorrow? I wanna make some beans in a couple o' days and need my pot. Usual time."

"Right on, my brother."

Plans made, they disconnected. David went and finished his now cold dinner before helping Sojourner with the kitchen.

Sean went back to his homework, cruising through the sheet like he'd never had a problem with it.

<hr>

"Ye Olde Brown Jug" had sat on the corner of Morton Street and Blue Hill Avenue as long as anyone in the neighborhood could remember, but no one called it by its full name. The pub went by The Brown Jug or by nothing at all. It wasn't fancy by any stretch of the term, but it had been a solid part of the once-Jewish neighborhood and served as a common watering hole.

David walked the four blocks to the pub and spotted Rome as soon as he pushed through the heavy wooden door. His friend sat at a booth near the back and waved him over. David passed the usual assortment of barflies and ne'er do wells from the neighborhood. He knew each and every one of them, nodding and slapping the occasional palm as he went.

Despite being a corner location, the pub was a narrow affair. One aisle split the space between bar and red-vinyl booths, the other between two more rows of booths behind a wall of thin wood columns. Yellow light and the haze of cigarette smoke made for a dim atmosphere amongst all the carved wood and intricate brass fittings.

Vinyl creaked as David slid in and bounced across the steel springs.

Rome pushed a frosted mug of beer in front of David and waited.

"Thanks, bruh." David sprinkled a pinch of salt into his beer and took a sip. He licked his lips and sighed. "Sean heard clicks on the phone."

Rome leaned back, his hands still around the mug in front of him. He kept his eyes downcast. "You hear 'em?"

David shook his head before taking another pull of beer.

"Could be nothin.'" Rome shrugged.

"Could be nothin.'" David nodded.

Rome drummed his fingers on his frosty mug. "Could be somethin' too."

"Could be somethin,'" David agreed.

Rome surveyed the small, dark bar. No one looked in their direction. "The BDP was a long time ago, m'man, ain't no reason for anyone to be tappin' phones today."

"I know. That's what's bugging me. It don't got to be about the BDP. We're Black. We were part of it. We'll always be targets." David feigned surprise. "Anyway, since when are you willing to let bygones be bygones?"

"Shiiiiit…" Rome grinned. "I'm not, but that ain't you. I'm paranoid as fuck about everything, all the time. You tell me Sean heard the clicks, even just once, and I'mma say someone's buggin' your phone. But that ain't *your* style, family man."

David smiled and snorted dismissively. Then he rubbed his eyes and said, "Well, today it's my style. I got too much to lose now and I want to get ahead of this, if I can. Your cousin—uh, Smitty, right? He still at City Hall?"

Rome took a drink while eyeing his friend. "Uh-huh."

"You think you could...?"

Rome sighed and said, "Yeah, sure, man. I'll see if he can find anything out. If these muthafuckas are back to their old tricks, might be a paper trail somewhere. Then again, might not. Could be they learned their lesson about paper trails."

"Yup."

"Watchu gonna do in the meantime, Dazz?"

"Well..." David finished his beer. "Gonna take a look 'round the house and the neighborhood and hope we ain't got any GIP sons o' bitches around. Maybe I can spot something."

"I still can't believe they called it the 'Ghetto Informants Program.'" Rome rolled his eyes.

"Yeah. Cruelty was their strong suit, not creativity." David shook his head.

"What about Sojourner, what're you gonna tell her?"

David blew out a lungful of air and ran his hands down his face. "I dunno. Yet. I mean, it's hard to tell when she's picked up on something or what she's thinking. Her timing's always been different, you know."

"So ask."

"Not until I know more. I don't want to set something off, if there's nothing to be worried about."

"She was right in the middle of that shit with us, just before the end, man. I know she was the most militant among us."

David sighed and leaned back. "I know. It's just... I don't think she dwells on it. You know? She kind of travels in her own circles. Anyway..."

The two men stood, shook hands and embraced. David dropped a five-dollar bill on the table and said his goodbyes on the way out.

Rome watched his friend leave, the old tension building in his chest; he was sure it wouldn't make him feel a little better to have his paranoia validated. Not at the expense of David's family. He scooped up the five, left two dollars on the table, and made a call from the payphone in the back.

Summer came early and life was filled with odd days of warmth and rain. There'd been so much precipitation over the winter, patches of snow remained here and there, but it wasn't cold enough to wear coats and gloves. It made for some interesting and dangerous snowball fights. You could never be sure if it was just snow or an ice brick or something worse, like a rock.

Sean loved summer. It meant warm breezes, swimming, his birthday, away camp, and long empty days that could include both reading and physical fun. He'd left his windows open last night and the room was chilly. It was a welcome chill, however, one that carried freshness into the room. Once the neighborhood fully thawed, the stink of dog droppings and uncapped garbage cans could sneak up a nose.

He rolled out of bed and dressed quickly. It was early and school was out; no need to be up, but he wanted to catch his father before he left for work.

David was on the phone, in the kitchen, speaking in low tones. Sojourner was still in bed. Sean leaned in the doorway, waiting. He'd almost missed his father's exit. David had his jacket on and his soft briefcase leaned against his leg. He disconnected the call and turned to his son.

"Morning, Sean," he said with a smile.

Sean grinned and hugged his father. "I wanted to catch you before you left for work. You're going in early a lot."

David nodded. "Best time to get done what I need to get done. Not a lot of folks come in early. I'll be home for dinner." He slapped Sean's back affectionately and leaned back. "You stink, Son. Take a shower."

"Dad…"

"Bathe, boy. Get clean before your mother wakes up, it's time you paid more attention to that, you're growing up. Them stink glands come with that." David gave his son a gentle push. "I gotta go, love you."

"I love you too, Dad."

David scooped up his bag, walked quickly down the hall, and left. Things were different, somehow, had been different since the end of winter. Sean noticed, but he didn't have the information to connect any dots in his father's private life. All he could observe was his attitude around the house, how distracted and slightly withdrawn he seemed.

Sean ruffled his shirt a few times and sniffed his armpits. He looked at the bathroom and sighed, resigned.

Before he entered, his mother called out, "Sean?"

"Yeah, Mom?"

"What do you want for breakfast?"

"Uh… Cream o' wheat! With bacon!"

"And toast?"

"Yes, four slices, please!"

Sean waited.

"That's… a bit much."

"Pleeeeeeaaase?"

He heard his mother sigh and roll out of bed.

"Thank you, Mummy!"

She groaned in response, her impression of Karloff's "Mummy" from the old movie.

After showering and getting dressed and, a new habit, remembering to paste on deodorant, Sean hustled into the kitchen. A bowl of hot cereal waited, with a pad of melting butter at its center. While his mother cleaned up the pans, Sean shoveled sugar and crumbled bacon into the wheat. Then he scooped the mixture into his mouth using the toast.

Sojourner shook her head. "You're going to eat us out of this home. It's a wonder you're not fat."

Sean shrugged, focused on breakfast. "It's delicious, Mom."

She smiled, "You're welcome, my prince."

Today was his day to invite friends to his birthday barbecue at Franklin Park this weekend. He hoped his mother wouldn't put on a show of calling him that in front of them. He hoped his father wouldn't be working.

"Hey, Mom, why's Dad working so much, what's he doing?"

Sojourner paused. She didn't look at her son, but answered, "It's just extra stuff. It comes up every other year or so."

Sean's face betrayed his confusion, but his mother, her back turned, hadn't seen. He let it go, choosing instead to think it through on his own. When his mother got vague, that's where she stayed for the duration. If he was going to get answers from her, he'd have to wait for another time when she was more relaxed about his questions. He thought back to past years—not that many— he hadn't paid attention to his father's work until recently. He always remembered being happy when his father came home, running to greet him. Going to work early and coming home late were not things he remembered.

Time only started to matter recently.

Mike jogged across the street, joining the gang. The four of them were heading to the rink. Mike had never been and he was nervous.

"Hey, fellas," Mike said as he mounted the sidewalk. "How many times y'all been to this place?"

"It's been here as long as me and Gerry can remember. We've sort of always gone, every now and then."

Gerry nodded.

The rink was the premier skating location for the trifecta of Boston's Black neighborhoods. Everyone skated there. *Everyone.* Most girls owned their own skates and wherever girls went, boys followed. The trouble was that none of Sean's friends could skate competently. Sean's older cousin taught him whenever he visited his aunt's home in Roxbury—which was frequent. Still, having eight wheels on his feet had never felt comfortable.

Mike said, "And there's a lot of girls that hang out there?" He kept pushing his glasses back up his nose.

"I hope so," DJ replied. His voice brayed as he skipped and bounced around the group.

"Ha," Gerry said. "You ain't gonna talk to no girls."

"Watch me!"

Sean said, "I hope all that energy keeps you upright long enough."

"Yeah, I got that energy!" DJ humped the air a few times, his legs spread in a dynamic pose.

The rest of the boys groaned. If any of them did get a chance to talk to a girl, chances were high that DJ's enthusiasm would make a mess of things.

"Oh, hey," Sean said, "can y'all make it to my birthday party or what?"

A chorus of 'yes' in various forms came at him.

"Cool!"

"Wouldn't miss it for the world, my prince," DJ said.

"Shut up, man!" Sean swiped at DJ, who skittered away. He glanced at Mike. "And you. Don't be so nervous."

"Easy for you to say."

"Easy for me to say to you."

Mike looked confused. "What's that even mean?"

Sean shrugged. "I'm nervous too. I just hide it better. *You* need some paper towels."

Mike sighed and used his shirt to mop sweat off his face.

Chez Vous nestled diagonally across the intersection of Morton and Blue Hill. The streets were large enough to make crossing them more dangerous than not, but the promise of music, girls, and a dark room beckoned. Sean double-checked his pocket. He had just enough to get in and rent skates. There'd be no snacks or drinks.

"Everybody got money for the ticket *and* rental?"

They all nodded.

"Here we go."

Outside the entrance, a short line had formed and the thump of music could be heard. Some days the place was full of young kids—single-digit ages. Older teenagers dominated the late evening. There was a sweet spot between when kids Sean's age might gather. There were no set times or special events for emerging teens, so it was organic, entirely up to chance. Either the place was full of girls the right age or younger kids and their adult chaperones.

They got lucky.

Inside, lights flashed and the thump of music drowned out the thunder of rollerskates on polished wood. Groups of boys and girls were scattered around the carpet outside the rink, but only mingled on the skating floor. The odor of cheap cologne and sweat hung over the entire affair.

Disco lights nagged at something in the back of Sean's brain. As distracting as they were, the colors didn't detract from all the girls laughing and skating. A couple of groups were working on dance moves, syncing their bodies to the beat on wheels.

"Oh, wow!" DJ spared a few looks towards the hardwood before beating feet to the rental counter. He kept repeating the word, 'wow,' until he was out of earshot.

The boys all exchanged glances and Gerry said, "Hey, he's got the right idea. Let's roll!"

Sean nudged Mike. "Corny?"

Mike nodded. "Corny."

Both boys pointed at Gerry and said, "Corny!"

By the time the three of them had rental skates in hand, DJ had finished lacing his up and was stumbling toward the wood.

"Yo, hold up, DJ," Sean said.

"A man with a plan, fellas, a man—" he stumbled, his skates caught on the carpet for a moment "—with a plan."

"What the hell's he talking about?" Gerry asked.

Mike and Sean shrugged as DJ clutched the edges of the entrance and launched himself onto the floor. He pinwheeled his arms and ran in place, making little progress.

The boys guffawed. DJ looked like he was skating on an electric current the way his limbs jerked. Inwardly, they marveled at his bravery. Sean stole glances as he laced his skates up. His obnoxious friend showed nothing but raw determination and no grace at all. His twitching and stumbling form had made it halfway around the rink by the time the rest of them got on the floor.

Gerry and Mike proved competent, but slow, skating like the novices they were. Etiquette demanded that they stay along the walls, leaving room for the faster, more skilled skaters around the center. DJ struggled with the concept, and more skilled skaters parted around him. Sean hung back with the others while remembering the advice his cousin had given him about rollerskates. She'd grown up on the rattling metal-wheeled kind, navigating asphalt and concrete in the Roxbury housing co-op where she lived. A skating rink was a rarified luxury.

Flex your knees, See-Anne, just lean left and right and you'll go! You gotta find your balance and be confident.

She always called him that. See-Anne. It didn't bother him, though, it was good advice and she was otherwise always kind to him like a caring, older sister.

Ahead of them, DJ nearly crashed into a group of girls. He yelled, "Oh, no, I'm sorry!" before spinning to the floor in a heap, cutting them off. The girls laughed at him and skated around, but one broke off and helped DJ up. She started to give him pointers, then escorted him along.

"Look at that," Gerry said.

"Yeah," Mike said. "Look at that. Y'know, that girl was showing her friends how to skate. I don't think DJ did that on accident."

"Sunnuvabitch," Sean muttered, "'a man with a plan.'"

Just then, Peanut shot by, skating backward.

One of Gerry's legs snapped into the air and he lost balance, sitting down hard.

"Oh, sorry, bruh," Peanut said and rocketed around the bend.

Mike took one of Gerry's arms and Sean the other.

"He did that on purpose," Sean said as he helped Gerry to his feet.

Gerry just moaned in response.

"You okay?"

"Yeah, Mike, I just… I just need a minute." Gerry rubbed his tailbone.

As they guided Gerry to the floor exit, Sean heard DJ's cackle. His friend glided by, skating like a stiff, and still chatting with the girl who'd helped him up. He couldn't be bothered with anything else happening around him. Gerry took a seat and Sean looked back to the floor. Peanut was making another round. He zoomed up behind DJ and his new friend, then he feinted like he was going to pat the girl's bottom. At the last moment, he spun, grinning, and pointed back at his friends. Then he nodded and pointed at himself.

Sean had seen enough.

Dickhead, Sean thought. A hot rush of blood made his jaw clench. His ears thrummed with an unfamiliar feeling and the scene inside the building fell deeper into focus.

One of the roller refs gave two short blasts on their

whistle and said, "Slow it down, young man, that's your second warning."

"Yo, where you goin'?"

Sean heard Mike's question clearly over the cacophony of music and voices. But he ignored the question, keeping his eyes on Peanut. The boy had nodded, largely ignoring the ref, and checked his speed. A little. Sean entered the floor and leaned in toward the middle. The air rushing past him felt like a language all itself. Every gust and swirl told a story of where everybody was, how fast they were going, and what size they were. The walls were a dead space, the inner ring swirled slower than the outer ring of skaters.

Peanut surged around as Sean picked up speed. The second time his target came up behind him, Sean recognized the story the air told, he could feel it on the back of his neck and head.

As Peanut passed, Sean stepped into his tailwind, mimicking the boy's moves. It didn't take long for Peanut to notice he had a trailer. Dom, off the rink floor, slapped the shoulder of Peanut's other friends and pointed. Peanut picked up speed and Sean matched it, pulling closer to him. They cut across lanes and Sean got closer still until his skates were nearly touching Peanut's. The boy growled, lurched, and spun to skate backward. Sean matched the move, staying glued to Peanut as if they'd worked out a routine in advance.

"Hey, get the fuck off me," Peanut snarled.

A ref gave two short blasts and said, "Slow it down you two! And you," he pointed at Peanut, "You're done, get off the floor."

Peanut sucked his teeth and spun again. Sean stayed with him and let one of his skates connect with Peanut's wheels. Sean expected it, Peanut didn't, and the boy sprawled hard onto the shining planks.

"Oh, sorry, bruh," Sean said, stopping to offer his hand.

Peanut glared and reached up.

Sean skated backward. "Psych."

Peanut smacked the floor and flipped him the bird.

The ref stopped next to Peanut and helped him up. "I was only going to put you off the floor, but now you gotta go. Out, all the way out!"

Peanut pointed at Sean and said, "Yo, I'mma see you outside, bitch!"

"Hey, don't look at him, look at me: get out!" The ref escorted Peanut to the exit. Dom and the others protested, loudly. "Your friends too! All o' you, out!" He waved his arms, herding them towards the exit, allowing them to unlace and collect their shoes.

The circling skaters all slowed to watch events unfold. Mike skated up and remained abreast with Sean.

"What the hell, man? You never said you could skate like that! Holy shit, what now? They gonna kick your ass when you leave."

"*My* ass? You ain't got my back?"

Mike sighed, met Sean's eyes, and said, "O' course, man, don't be like that." Then he mumbled, "Ain't fair you gettin' us all in trouble like that, though."

"I'll get us out, then."

DJ skated up. "Yooooo, what the fuck you do, Sean?"

"You two get Gerry and meet me at the counter so we can all get our shoes together."

"What? Noooo! This girl—"

"You missed what happened," Sean said, "what Peanut did to Gerry."

"I saw you zippin' around behind Peanut. When you learn to skate like that and why we all gotta go?"

"Because I'm not letting Peanut and his boys kick my ass and if they don't get me, they gonna get you."

DJ blinked twice and made up his mind to cooperate.

The two boys caught up with Gerry. Behind them, the floor's gyre cranked back up, and within minutes, the rink was back to normal operation.

"Did y'all see that? Man, Peanut busted his ass! When the hell did Sean learn to skate like that?" Gerry wavered between glee and sorrow. "Peanut's gonna *kill* Sean. Where is he?"

"Yeah, we saw," Mike said, "Sean told us to meet him at the counter."

"What? We leavin'?"

Mike and DJ looked at each other and shrugged.

"But Peanut's gonna be waitin' for him outside. Shit, he's gonna be waitin' for *all of us*." Gerry threw his hands up and shook his head. "What the hell was Scan thinking?"

"I don't know," Mike said. "C'mon, let's find out."

The trio collected their shoes and looked out for Sean. After a few minutes of their rubbernecking, Sean slipped from the crowd. He already had his shoes on.

Gerry asked, "Where you been?"

"Listen—"

Gerry stepped in front of Sean. "What is going—"

"*Listen*. We can't just wait 'til closing or walk out the front."

"Oh, no," Mike said.

"What?" DJ's face contorted into a comical, confused mess.

"We can't walk together, but we all gotta be near the emergency exit."

"But the alarm will—"

"That don't matter. We all rush the door and we all hotfoot back to my street. Take the long way, down Blue Hill Ave and cross after the corner store."

"I don't know," Mike said.

"I'll open the door, that'll be on me. Okay? Listen, I'll crash the door. Then DJ, then Mike, then Gerry. Boom, boom, boom. We can't be trippin' over each other."

DJ asked, "Why that order, why I gotta go first?"

Without missing a beat, Sean said, "Because you're the fastest."

"Oh. Uh, okay." DJ struggled with this news.

Gerry and Mike shared a look. They understood that DJ would freak out first, regardless. He needed to be out and pounding pavement before anyone else.

"Just remember: we can't draw attention going over there. If the ref or someone notices, we'll get busted. Okay?"

Everyone nodded.

"We go in pairs, opposite directions, split up halfway so we by ourselves. Gerry, with me. Let's go."

Before anyone could protest, Sean started moving. Gerry followed in his wake. He didn't look back to see if anyone else moved.

"Thanks," Gerry said to the back of Sean's head.

Sean nodded in response and kept moving. On the other side of the rink, he paused, facing inward, watching some of the girls skate. One of them smiled in his direction as she skated past, pointing and giggling with her friend. Sean felt an urge to run and get his skates again. He stayed in place, riding the thrill of possibilities, waiting to be sure everyone was in position.

Peanut just needed time to simmer down. There

was no need for direct conflict after this. There'd be some tit-for-tat later, Sean was sure. For now, however, he turned and hit the crash bar as hard as he could. A high-pitched alarm sounded and light from outside flooded into the rink. DJ shot past him like a grouse from high grass, cackling his bird-like laugh. The others followed and they all sprinted into the neighborhood.

The big day came like any other.

Birthday parties weren't a regular feature in the family, but Sean's happened to coincide with peak summer. There weren't any presents, not like on TV, just a gathering and whatever fun could be squeezed out of being together. Most of the family was there: aunts, uncles, cousins. And friends, some friends of family, people he'd always thought of as cousins or aunts were there as well. Franklin Park hosted the event. They were on the southern edge of the golf course, full of rolling hills, perfect for flying a kite. Sighting a golfer was a rare occasion. The park made for poor golfing as no one respected play.

The smell of the grill, at the edge of the field, permeated the air while Sean struggled to keep a kite aloft. He was flanked by two much older cousins, each of them holding a beer. Gerry stood nearby; he'd helped get the bat-shaped thing into the sky.

"You're thirteen now," OC said.

His real name was James, but everyone called him "OC." It was from something that happened in Vietnam, but no one ever explained it.

Sean tugged on the kite string, balancing at the edge

of the hill. "Uh, yeah?" Out of the corner of his eye, he could see OC grinning and nodding to Pick.

Pick said, "Yeah, Cuz, how come you didn't invite your girlfriend?"

Pick was an easy nickname to understand, his last name was "Pickney," though he preferred if people believed it was a sobriquet about basketball skills.

"Well…" Sean stammered a bit.

OC and Pick laughed, clinked bottles, and slapped Sean on the back.

Sean laughed nervously and spared a moment to focus on Pick. He chucked his shoulder and said, "Why didn't you invite yours?"

OC, in the midst of drinking from his bottle, sputtered.

Pick smirked. "When you get to be my age, you'll know the answer to that question." He raised his bottle and waggled it. "I'm out. Another?"

OC drained his bottle and said, "Let's do it."

"Happy birthday, cousin," Pick said to Sean. "We'll see you at the table. Your pop gotta be done with the burgers by now."

OC chimed in, "Man does not live by potato salad alone!"

"Why does your mom burn the hot dogs?" Pick asked.

Sean opened his mouth—

"Don't answer that. C'mon, Pick, let that boy alone."

They meandered back to the picnic area.

"Well, that was embarrassing," Gerry said.

"For who?" Sean asked.

"Whichever. Hey, man, I'm hungry. There's Mike and DJ! C'mon, let's eat."

Sean glanced over his shoulder. "Go start a plate. I'll

be right behind you after I reel this thing in." Sean began winding the kite string up, thinking about what OC and Pick had been hassling him about.

Messy dreams had crept into his nights long ago. Dreams about girls he knew from school or around the neighborhood. Physical stuff. Sex stuff. It wasn't something he talked about with friends—none of them talked about it. Girls weren't a regular feature in his life, but they'd become as impossible to ignore as the intense, daily erections.

Sean finished wrapping the kite up and started walking back to the picnic tables. His mother waved when she saw him coming. "I made a plate for you, my prince," she called.

Sean froze. Everyone within earshot laughed and shook their heads about David's strange wife.

Everyone enjoyed the park until sundown.

Part Five: Disclosures

Sean had pocket money after his birthday, and other than books or comics, he wanted to pick up an album downtown. Sojourner had been listening to Noel Pointer, EW&F, and a classical piano composition—he had no idea what it was—on heavy rotation. As good as all of it was, as lush and warm and funky, as much as it spoke musically to him, he was interested in something less polished. Rougher. A sound that was stirring a nascent love in him. He'd caught snatches of "Red Hot Mama" on the radio late one night after dinner at cousin Pick's house. The hardest part had been finding out who the band was. He hadn't heard the DJ's introduction over all the conversation, but Pick knew the song. Needing to sing part of it to him had been humiliating, but worth it. With the track identified, it took a few phone calls to the radio station in order to identify the album itself. That the song was a remake of a composition originally recorded by Parliament, a closely associated band, exacerbated the problem, but now the hunt for Funkadelic's album, *Standing On The Verge Of Getting It On*, was afoot.

He didn't find the LP until the third record store, about four blocks from his father's office. Sean was the only customer in the small shop and released a breathy exclamation upon locating the album. He walked up to the counter, a grin on his face.

The cashier, a tall, slim Black man wearing tight denims, ornate leather cuffs, and a goatee trimmed to a deft point, looked at the LP and said, "Oh, you likes the funk, eh?"

Sean nodded, "I do."

"Yeah, little brother, *if* you do—"

"*I do.*"

"Cool. This the real funk, but you gotta check this out." The cashier pulled a record out of the used bin on top of the counter and handed it to Sean.

He read the sleeve. "'*Soul Makossa*. The Lafayette Afro Rock Band'? Never heard of 'em."

"You'll dig it, little brother."

Sean's face scrunched. "But it's used." He held the album out to the cashier.

The tall fellow shook his head, refusing to take the disc. "It's *loved*. Trust me, little brother, I cleaned and tested that record myself. Look here," he tapped the top left corner, "'S only fifty cents."

"I ain't never heard them on the radio."

"Probably won't and you gonna want the next one after you listen to it. This is Boston, m'man, we ain't cool enough for this here. Maybe you cool enough, though. I'd spin it for you, but the player's in the shop. Come back, if you dig it, check out the others."

"What if I don't?"

The clerk smiled.

Sean dropped an extra fifty cents on the counter.

Despite the length of the hunt, he was still going to

have at least a half-hour wait until his father left work. Which meant he had some time to visit the "bookstore" under the elevated tracks on Washington Street. The sky had darkened, rain was coming. He could smell it in the air, the moisture of gravid clouds and ozone that promised lightning. There was a light sheen of sweat on his body from the walk and he was thankful for the shrink-wrap and plastic bag protecting his purchase.

The destination wasn't really a bookstore, but he called it that for the amount of comics and books kept in a cardboard box near the front of the shop. The place carried all sorts of bric-a-brac, but only the boxes held Sean's attention. Inside, the atmosphere was no less muggy. Without air-conditioning, the smell of mass-printed paper overwhelmed the cramped space. The man behind the counter, with sandy skin, thick hair, and a horseshoe mustache, nodded at Sean when their eyes met. Sean nodded back. Neither of them betrayed emotion on their faces.

The boxes were industrial-sized, no doubt used for holding some commercial refrigerators or freezers. Now they each held scores of pocket-sized books, all with their covers sheared off. It made the hunt all the richer, however, because one had to dig to find gems. Comics were ten cents apiece and books twenty. It was a treasure trove of stories, if one could find something interesting to read. Outside, the train roared into the station and hundreds of footsteps echoed down the metal stairs shortly thereafter. Shadows of passersby flitted outside the storefront's filthy windows.

Sean rooted around in the box, trying his best to decide which paperbacks would be worthwhile, until he found a hardback bound in orange cloth with a blue spine and gold type. It was rare to find anything other than mass-market paperbacks in the box. He felt a thrill of discovery as he read the spine: *The Man Who Folded Himself*. He'd never read David Gerrold and the hardcover had no descriptive information without its dust cover. He resolved to give this one a try because of its physical rarity. To make the trip worthwhile, he collected a few comics, as well, featuring illustrators he was familiar with. Sixty cents later, he was on the way around the corner to meet his father and keeping a wary eye on the sky.

When Sean turned the corner onto the street his father's office lay, he nearly ran into David.

"Whoah! I was coming to the store to find you, boy."

"Hi, Dad!" Sean awkwardly hugged his father, keeping hold of his prizes in clenched fingers.

David put one arm around Scan's shoulders, his valise in the other hand, and led him across the street.

"What'd you get, anything I'd know?"

"Uh…"

"Never mind, I don't wanna know." David smiled. "C'mon, looks like it's gonna rain. I'm parked about a block over. Let's hustle."

Father and son took long strides to the heavy, powder blue Chevrolet his father drove. The first drops spattered the windshield as soon as they'd taken a seat on the bench. David flipped on the wipers and cranked the thing into gear. Sean always felt like he was floating when riding in the car.

"Dad, how did you meet Mom?"

David made an inconclusive sound that felt like a dismissal to Sean. His heart dropped a few inches.

"Well," David said, rubbing one hand across his face, "we met while I was working at the BDP. I thought Uncle Rome told you?"

"I mean, he said there was a bomb—"

"Okay, listen." David sighed before he went on. "Our time with the Black Defense Program was… great and worthwhile until it suddenly wasn't. It became dangerous because our government only appears to be 'out of many, one' when in reality it's to benefit a few."

"You mean, white people?"

"White *men* in particular, yes. And working with the BDP was a way to escape that, for a while, and to help people. *Our* people." David emphasized his words by indicating himself and Sean. "The better we got at what we did, the more scrutiny we came under until the FBI got involved."

"What'd you do with them? The BDP?"

David smiled. "I was part of the educational outreach effort. I helped create supplementary weekend curricula for middle- and high-school classes. I tutored too. That's why Rome calls me the 'Minister of Knowledge' sometimes." He shook his head, a wry smile playing on his lips. "All that because I read a lot and had some aptitude with math."

"What did Mom do with the BDP?"

"Ah. She, uh, mostly did volunteer work. Just helping out where needed."

"So, you met Mom at a bombing?"

David winced. "Kind of. There were several of us supporting a protest downtown. Right down there, near the Financial District. It was a multicultural and multi-organizational effort, lots of volunteers. It was a different time, more…" David grasped at the words. "More, uh, an attitude that love conquers and all that. Hippie stuff.

The BDP wasn't exactly militant, just dedicated to the uplift of colored folks. Anyhow, we don't know if it was an accident or one of the other groups, or if it was COINTELPRO. All I know is there was an explosion and it hurt a bunch of folks. Your mom included."

"Wow," Sean said.

"Yeah. It was like a giant clapped his hands on everyone. Your mom was just suddenly there, in front of me, and I grabbed her. Rome helped, after that. We all got out of there alive. That's it."

"That's it?"

"What were you expecting?"

Sean grit his teeth and looked out the window. "I don't know. We don't know anyone on Mom's side of the family and you and Rome are the only ones who knew her before I came along."

"Sojourner lost her family before she met me."

"In the bombing?"

"No. Before that. Y'know, violence is nothing like the movies, Son. It's sudden and scary. People get hurt, they heal, they change. If they survive. You either pick up and move on or get ground under it. We moved on. Together."

"Okay, Dad." Sean nodded at his father before turning back to watch the rain-soaked streets of Boston morph from downtown streets to their own. A strange mix of fear and longing twisted in Sean's gut. He couldn't let it go, everything felt like a big secret even when it wasn't.

***

It was the end of the week and Sean had two things on his mind: dinner and getting back to the record store. In the weeks since meeting his father downtown, he'd spun the record to death.

Sojourner put the lid on the biggest cast iron pan they had. Inside, chicken stewed. Along with the chicken, a pot of rice simmered and green beans steamed. One of Sean's favorite meals. He curled up in the living room with the hardback book he'd bought downtown, anticipating dinner.

A glance at the clock confirmed that his father was late. Sean closed the book and wandered into the kitchen.

"Is Dad working late?"

Humming over the big pan, Sojourner nodded.

"Is dinner almost done?"

She smiled and said, "Yes, my prince, not long now."

Sean rolled his eyes and strolled out of the kitchen. He heard his mother's soft laughter behind him. He looked out the front windows. The street lamps were flickering on as the sun set, smearing a brilliant set of colors from yellow to blue to red and purple. Across the street, from this view, it was clear how closely the tripledeckers were placed.

Outside, it never seemed that way, with space between each of them to run along. Most of the apartment buildings stood on feet of puddingstone above basements deep enough to stand in. The foundations reminded Sean of a nightmare he'd had where puddingstone monsters melted from the foundations and invaded the neighborhood. The sky burned the entire time as if the clouds were on fire. It had been terrifying. Though not as terrifying as the night he dreamed a tyrannosaurus rex walked down the street, late at night, peering in windows. He'd hid on the floor, under the sill, too afraid to look and see if the beast had moved on.

As he thought of beasts made of stone and flesh, his father's blue Chevy pulled up to the driveway. The car couldn't make the turn, another vehicle was parked too close. David hopped out of the car and opened the green fence. He spoke briefly to someone out of Sean's view—probably a neighbor—before they ran out and moved the car. Sean knew his father hated when people parked in or too near their driveway. He hoped Dad wouldn't be irritable when he came in.

Feeling a little too old to rush into his father's arms when he walked through the door, Sean opted to plop down on the couch and call out, "Hey, Dad! You're just in time for dinner."

David poked his head into the living room, a tightness around his eyes, and smiled at his son. "Just gotta put all this stuff down and we can eat."

Sean clapped his hands and headed for the kitchen.

In the hallway, David lingered, composing himself. He could see his son's future now, the break from parents, moving towards full independence. This was when it started, as the overflow of unconditional love throttled back. Rather than give in to the melancholy with sighs and sagging shoulders, David took a deep breath and quietly let it out. This was normal and normal was what he wanted. It was what he and Sojourner planned for, the life she assured him they could lead. He could deal with the problems coming at them from outside, he still had friends who understood that much, certainly.

David washed his hands and stepped into the kitchen. The usual clatter of plates and silverware preceded the meal to come. He hugged and kissed Sojourner from behind before sitting down. Sean sat across from David and rubbed his hands in anticipation, a comical leer on his face.

"Wash your hands, boy."

"I did!"

David pointed at the bathroom.

"You didn't even ask whether I had already."

David leaned on the table and grinned. "Because I know you didn't."

"That's 'cause I forgot!" Sean hustled out of the kitchen and into the bathroom.

Sojourner lay a steaming plate of the chicken on rice with green beans where Sean had been seated. She smiled at David. "I should say you're too hard on him, but you're not."

"True." David shrugged. "How was your day, did you get much done?"

"I did. You?"

David crossed his arms, putting his chin in one hand and nodded. "I think so."

"More late nights to come?"

David sighed and smoothed his lap. "Not much more, I don't think."

"Good."

Sean returned and dug in.

"Careful, my prince, it's hot."

"Mom, you gotta stop calling me that." He pushed a fork full of steaming meat into his mouth and immediately regretted it.

David smirked, gently blowing on his own speared meat.

Sojourner said, "I cannot, it's the truth."

"Moooommm…"

"You're the son of a queen. Ask your father."

David gave a shrug in a what-can-I-say manner, not making eye contact.

"Hey, Dad?"

"Yeah," David answered around a mouthful of food.

"Can I have five bucks for this weekend?"

David arched an eyebrow. "Hm. Movies?"

"Yeah."

"Sure. You goin' with Gerry and Mike?" David dragged his wallet out of a back pocket and slipped a five-dollar bill to his son.

"And DJ and maybe Cole."

David grinned. "That's a lotta trouble headin' downtown."

Sean rolled his eyes. "Hardly." He tucked the bill into his pocket. "Thanks, Dad!"

"What are you going to see?" Sojourner asked.

"*Cooley High*. It was Gerry's idea."

David chuckled. "That'd explain why it's not monsters or aliens."

All the good stuff is R-rated anyway. At least it isn't 'Grease,' Sean thought.

Sean met Gerry at the corner of their street. Of all his friends, Gerry lived the closest.

"Yo."

"'Sup."

They walked the four blocks to Blue Hill Avenue in comfortable silence. The two of them had known each other for nearly all their lives and not every moment needed to be filled with conversation. They crossed the big curve in Morton Street and waited at the corner for the bus that would take them to Egleston Square. It'd be easier to catch a bus closer to home and go to Forest Hills, but DJ was coming from Mattapan Square and they'd see him on the bus or at the elevated station going downtown.

"I'm hungry."

Sean looked at his friend. Two years older and a beanpole. "You didn't eat breakfast?"

"I had some cereal."

Sean's mother had prepared scrambled eggs, bacon, and toast. The more he learned how other kids ate, the odder he felt. "Get something in the corner store, it's right there."

"Naw. Here comes the bus. I'll get something down-town, my dad gave me a ten."

"Ten dollars?" Sean was surprised. "Must've been a good night in the cab."

Gerry shrugged. "I guess so. I think he just wanted me out of the house for the day."

"Damn, I only have five." It was enough for a movie and maybe a snack at McDonald's; it wouldn't last the whole day.

Gerry's family lived in a narrow apartment, Sean knew, with Gerry at the back, off the kitchen and his parents up front. It was a triple-decker that'd been split in half to double its occupancy. Technically a one-bedroom apartment, Gerry could hole up for days, listening to records. It made sense that his parents would take advantage of the time.

The bus pulled up, disgorged a few passengers, and the boys stepped on. They each dropped a dime into the coin box. They could see DJ, a big grin on his face, seated all the way in the back. The bus was largely empty, late morning on a Saturday.

After a few daps by way of greeting, DJ asked, "Yo, Ger, what's this movie about, man?"

Gerry shrugged again, living up to his reputation as a low-key cat and uttered one word. "Us."

Sean rolled his eyes.

DJ said, "You mean 'cause it's Black folks?"

Gerry shrugged yet again. "Sure."

"That's it? 'Sure'? You *sure*, brothah?" DJ cackled.

"High school, man, brothers tryin' to find a way is all, and it looks funny."

"It's a comedy," Sean piped in.

"Sure," Gerry said.

DJ and Sean exchanged a look and a laugh at Gerry's expense. The trio chatted along the way, about wherever they were on the ride. The fire at Chez Vous, the tennis program at Dorchester Field, the boring-ass Franklin Zoo, whether Skippy White's or Strawberries was the better record store, and finally Egleston Square where the elevated train met the Blue Hill Avenue bus line. The train stop was on the edge of a burgeoning Spanish-speaking population and at the center of a dirty mix of boarded-up businesses and gloomy stores that none of them frequented. Each of them dropped twenty cents into the slot and pushed through the turnstiles to wait for the train.

Sean asked, "Hey, any of y'all know anybody live down here?"

DJ said, "No."

Gerry shook his head. "I been down here a lot with my dad, when he's on shift. Just other people."

Sean said, "There ain't nothin' here. I been down on the street with my pops when he was makin' some rounds for—y'know, I don't know what the heck he was doing."

The other boys snickered. Sean knew his father worked in outreach and education. He organized, he knew lots of people, but… what was that, what was it called? Was it a profession, something to study for, aspire to? Sean himself was interested in comics and novels, movies and television. Stories. No one he knew of wrote or drew for any reason other than personal. He rarely saw anyone who looked like his family or friends doing that type of work. Every adult he knew either worked for the state as office workers or teachers or something equally dull. Mechanics, laborers, cleaners. All things he thought of as whatever jobs because adults treated the work that way.

Sean said, "Hey, Gerry, who made this movie?"

"Huh?"

"This movie, *Cooley High*, who made it?"

"Uhm, Michael Schultz, I think. He's the director."

"Black dude?"

Gerry looked lost for a moment and said, "I don't know."

The train roared into the station and the conversation carried on from there, but Sean tuned out until they arrived at the movie theater and things got interesting again.

They exited the theater laughing, well past their disappointment that Mike and Cole hadn't made it. In the midst of talking over his shoulder to DJ, Sean nearly walked into a girl whose head only came up to his chin.

By instinct, he put his hands up to her arms and steadied them both. "Oh, I'm sorry! I wasn't paying attention." He smiled, looking directly into her eyes.

They were green and he could see flecks of gold among emerald threads streaming towards the pupil and cascading deeper into her eyes. A universe of possibility swirled and plunged into those black holes. Energy spiraled and flashed, bits of power sparkled along the tips of his fingers and streaked through his body. He blinked, took a shaky breath, and released her.

"That's okay," she said.

Sean nodded, taking her in. She wore an off-white, striped knit that hugged her torso down to mid-hip. Her snug blue jeans tapered and billowed to white sneakers. Orange and gold stripes curved around her small, round breasts and slim waist. She had a cute, puckish nose and thick lips beneath it. Despite what looked like jet-black eyebrows, her hair was a deep reddish-brown and pulled into stiff puffs on either side of her head. Her light-brown skin was unblemished and glowed.

She said, "We was just going in to see *Cooley High*. Y'all seen it yet?"

Sean glanced at DJ and Gerry. Neither of them moved or said anything. The young woman had three friends with her, one dark-complected, the others somewhere between. None of them were as petite as she was, but they all looked pretty fine to Sean.

"Yeah, we just saw it. Funny flick, mostly, you'll like it," Sean said.

She grinned, "You don't know me. How you gonna know what I like?"

Something clicked in Sean's head. Maybe it was the last few hours relaxing with friends or watching the actors in the movie. Maybe it was the freedom of having a few dollars in his pocket, but thinking about it, he realized it was the mystery of the universe he saw in her eyes. And like a satellite on the edge of a gravity field, he'd been hooked.

Sean smiled back the same way she had and said, "My name's Sean. That's DJ and Gerry." His friends nodded and waved, still taken aback.

"I'm Donna. This is Peaches, Valerie, and Mia."

"Hey," her trio of friends said, in unison.

"All right," Sean said, "I'mma know what you like by gettin' to know you. See? Like this." He moved his hands to indicate the two of them.

Donna held back a smile. Sean's friends exchanged glances, wondering if this was the same boy they'd known for most of their lives. Donna's friends, for their part, pinched their lips and rolled their eyes.

An awkward and destructive pause rushed in. They were saved from that particular doom by the timely arrival of Mike and Cole.

"Hey!" The boys lit up, excited for the diversion of something familiar and comfortable.

After greetings, Sean said, "Y'all are late, but you get to meet Peaches, Valerie, Mia…" Sean paused, making eye contact with her before finishing. "… and Donna."

Mike and Cole, like Gerry and DJ, were stunned. They stood, shifting from foot to foot, keeping wary eyes on Sean.

"Anyway," Donna said, trailing off and turning to her friends.

Sean took one look at what was walking away and made an insistent face at his friends.

DJ screwed up his face and said, "Uh, what?"

"Mike and Cole need to see this flick," Sean answered.

Gerry seemed taken aback. "Are you tryin' to go watch it again?"

Sean glanced at Donna, she looked back and their eyes met for a moment. "Yeah, c'mon, I got just enough to get in again."

Mike shrugged and Cole said, "Cool!" The boys shook their heads and trailed in Sean's wake, he heard Gerry mutter, "Oh, my God," once.

It'd have made cartoonish sense if he floated two inches off the ground with his eyes closed and his nose in the air. As it was, Sean tried to comprehend what he was seeing. A cornucopia of color assaulted his eyes. Every shade in his view seemed dialed up to one hundred. He imagined he could see the air, but what it was, really, was that he could *feel* it. A tingle caressed his exposed skin, Donna's wake made a distinct impression. He could feel the shape of her, a tunnel in the atmosphere that he could follow.

None of the girls were interested in the fact that the boys were entering the theater with them. Donna seemed flattered, but she kept a cool head. For his part, Sean outwardly held it together while Donna's skin fairly glowed in his perception. They found seats together with their respective friends on either side of them.

Light bled off the screen, bathing the theater with a misty glow, like a fog of dry ice and pure color. Sean's eyes darted from left to right, trying to understand what he was seeing. The glow bent and curved, sparkled where it touched people and flowed around them. He curled into his seat, gripping the armrests, enthralled by the charged air. The sensations were so alien to him that he wasn't sure whether to be terrified or curious. All he could think was this was what an acid trip must be like. He'd never used drugs and wondered if Donna was seeing the same thing or if she'd done something to him somehow. In his eyes, Donna blazed next to him, a golden glow pinpricked with a rainbow of refractions that streaked from her pores. She turned her eyes to him, orbs of molten greens and white, and opened her mouth to speak, a cascade of colors spilled from her grinning lips.

"It's rude to stare," she said.

Sean's reverie broke, and the world as he'd known it for most of his life returned. "Sorry. I'd take a picture, if I had a camera."

Donna batted Sean's shoulder, a playful tap, and pointed at the screen.

He only gave half his attention to the movie.

The credits had rolled and all of them spilled from the theater. The two groups of teens walked into the Boston Common on what had become an aimless night. Neither group of friends had expected the day to turn out the way it had. There had been sporadic chatter between the two groups, but most of the conversation remained between established friends.

Sean and Donna only had eyes for each other. She pulled a pack of cigarettes out of her purse and sparked one up.

Sean, careful not to sound judgemental asked, "How long have you been smoking?"

Donna met his eyes and blew a stream of smoke discreetly from the corner of her mouth. "A couple years. You don't?"

Sean watched the smoke, a coiling cloud of darkness. To his eyes, it marred the pulsing rainbow of her essence. "No. Never tried. Don't care to."

"Huh," she answered. "You ever kiss a smoker?"

Without thinking, Sean said, "Not yet."

Donna winked and sprinted away, a trail of color and fading pinpoints of light in her wake obscured only by the cigarette smoke. Sean barely hesitated, not caring what his friends or anyone else thought. He took chase, skating through the tail of the beautiful comet he'd inexplicably snared. He could still feel the tingle of her skin where she'd brushed against him, the pressure of her knee against his, the gentle thump of her hand in the theater. Her tiny feet beat a faster rhythm than Sean's as he gave pursuit. She laughed and he drank the sounds in. When he closed the distance, she slowed down to a brisk walk. Neither of them were winded, a gift of youth.

"Why'd you run?" he asked, a laugh at the edge of his breath.

She flicked the cigarette away and grinned. Then she turned into him, raising her face to his. They kissed. She tasted of smoke and raw life. Her tongue danced against his and he gave in to impulse, running a hand around her waist to the small of her back, just above the curve that led to finer lands.

The rest of the group caught up to them, everyone wore a look of disapproval. One of Donna's friends pulled her away from Sean and said, "What's got into you?"

She laughed and playfully pushed her away.

They'd reached Charles Street and Sean felt a pang of caution. It hadn't been that long since whites rioted at City Hall, terrorizing any Black folks that came along. They'd attacked a Black attorney exiting the building and just the memory of the photo gave Sean chills. He saw a group of whites on Tremont Street, at the edge of the park, looking in their direction. Several boys and a few girls.

"I think we should head for the train," he said to them all.

As one, they recognized their safety in numbers. They headed for the Chinatown station for a train ride to Forest Hills where buses would take them to Mattapan and Roxbury. Some of the girls and boys got off at Dudley, leaving Donna with one exasperated friend fending off DJ's attempts at humor. Sean couldn't remember her name, she was the same one who'd questioned Donna. Gerry remained stoic. At Blue Hill Avenue, the boys divided.

Gerry said, "You forget where you live, Sean? We gotta cross the street."

Sean felt the few coins in his pocket and made a spontaneous decision. "Naw, I'm gonna see Donna home."

Gerry's eyes only widened a little. He nodded and said, "A'ight, see y'all later."

Donna said, "Bye," and Sean nodded.

DJ barely noticed, his attention still on Donna's friend. He lived near Mattapan Square, so he'd ride the bus to the end. The girls were points in-between. Sean wondered if DJ was even aware of how disinterested Mia was. Proud to have remembered her name, he mentioned it to Donna.

Sean leaned in, trying to ignore the hallucination of seeing her scent, and said quietly, "Your friend Mia don't seem all that interested in my boy DJ, does she?"

Donna snickered. "She got a boyfriend."

Sean smirked. "Maybe someone should let DJ know."

Donna glanced at the other pair. Mia made eye contact and pleaded with her face. Both Donna and Sean shrugged and laughed at their own synchronicity.

Mia fumed and DJ soldiered on until Mia exited the bus at her stop. She ran up the stairs of a triple-decker nearby, before the bus could pull too far away.

"Lucky she lives so close to the bus stop, on such a late night," Sean said.

DJ sucked his teeth and said, "I wish I'd gotten off too."

Sean rolled his eyes and Donna shot him a nasty look.

"No, that's not what I meant! I mean, my stop is almost last and I gotta walk like six blocks through these dark-ass streets before I can even see my place."

DJ sulked until Donna's stop. Sean gave his friend some dap before he exited with Donna. At that moment, if Sean had bothered to look back, he'd have seen DJ's incredulous expression.

They walked hand-in-hand and Sean's thoughts spun wild in several different directions at once. The electricity of her skin tingled bright orange in his sight. Her scent continued to waft rainbows around her. He couldn't bear it and had to speak, had to ruin the moment before it ruined him.

"Are you much further?"

"Next street," she said. "Why? You backin' out of walking me home?"

Sean snorted. "No. I… I'm just really glad I met you."

Donna smiled and her teeth lit up in cascading values of white. Then she said, "There is something—I don't know… My mom works nights and my aunt is away at some convention or another. You could come in." She looked down at their interlocked hands, and up into Sean's eyes.

He smiled in return and she giggled.

"You've never been with a girl like this, huh?"

Taken aback, he stuttered, completely unsure how to respond. She laughed and tilted her head and torso in a movement that sent Sean's senses spiraling even further. He pulled her in for a kiss, she came willingly, and when their lips met, time collapsed.

They were in the hallway.

They were inside the apartment.

They were in her room.

Sean was inside her.

He swam through a sea of candy colors, running his fingers through light that swam around his fingers like heavy gas. An unimaginable cascade of hues he couldn't identify drew him in and he hugged the brilliance to his bare chest. He ached with need, clutching at Donna, reveling in her embrace of him. They squirmed together, scrabbling at climax. Her hips bucked and the sound of her finishing reverberated off of Sean's skin, driving a shock of immeasurable pleasure through his body.

She pushed and he pulled away as he came. Rather than the viscous white mess he'd become accustomed to, his body sprayed something he'd never seen before. Sparks of the charged fluid ricocheted off of her swirling skin and faded from the brilliant blue and yellow tint of lightning to nothing at all.

They watched the fading bits in stunned silence. It left no discernible trace.

Donna's groan dragged Sean's attention back to what looked like a dreary, colorless reality. She made the sound again, a low and primal clench of breath before hissing, "What the fuck? What was all that?"

"I don't—"

Donna sat up. Her body trembled as she found her

voice. "The fuck is wrong with you? It's never been like that. You did something to me."

"I didn't—"

"Get out," she snarled.

"I'm sorry, I—"

"Get out!" She gathered up the covers, retreating further into the bed, away from him. She alternated between glaring at Sean and checking her body for traces.

Sean dressed and left. It was going to be a long, drab walk home alone with his thoughts.

Part Six: Fears Abound

The neighborhood was dead silent, as expected. To say he was disappointed was an understatement. Nothing felt right. The past hour, the current hour, his own body. What had it been that had come out of him? The question ran through whatever other thought he had. The discharge looked nothing like what the boys had seen in stacks of crumpled magazines behind garages, or the results of his own private explorations. This was new and different and *bad*.

The environment seemed dead to his senses, a pall of dull colors, nothing like what it had been with Donna. He felt electrified and numb at the same time, putting one foot in front of the other to chew up the nearly two miles between him and home. With any luck, he'd be able to slip in and go to bed with no one the wiser.

He was not lucky.

David and Sojourner waited. Sean's father paced and his mother sat on the couch. David had been drinking—not drunk, but Sean could smell the difference, an alcohol-tinged energy rode David's demeanor. He was the first to speak.

"Where the fuck have you been, boy?"

Sean met his mother's eyes for a moment. Sojourner's eyes narrowed and she tilted her head back, as if to smell the air of failure around Sean.

"Don't look to your mother, I asked you a question."

Sean fidgeted, feeling none of the confidence he'd been riding earlier. Back then it had been as if he knew what he needed to do and how to do it. Now, he stumbled over his words, and thoughts came in fragments, if at all.

David's harangue reached a more urgent pitch.

Sojourner interjected quietly. "Who were you with?"

David paused.

Sean took a deep breath and said, "DJ, Gerry, and later on, Mike and Cole."

David stared at his wife, trying to understand her angle.

"Who else?" Sojourner asked, tilting her head.

"I... uh, we met some girls."

David appeared taken aback, an incredulous look danced around his eyes. He said, "And?"

"I walked one of them home, but I didn't have enough change to take the bus back. She lives near Mattapan Square."

Sojourner took a deep breath, folded her hands in her lap, and went still. David tilted his head and said, "Go to your room, go to bed. Just go on now." All of his anger hissed out in the command.

Sean went to his room and eased the door shut.

"Can you believe this boy? I didn't think he'd pull something like this for another couple of years. It's not like him." He had more words that wouldn't sort out his thoughts, but no one to speak them to. His wife wasn't paying attention to him.

Sojourner didn't answer or look at David. She remained still.

David sat on the ottoman in front of his wife. He looked into her eyes, but she was somewhere else, looking through him to some other thoughts. He took her hands in his and she focused on him.

"Sojourner, what is it? Do you think—"

"I don't know." She squeezed her husband's hands and stood up. "I'm going to go and speak with him."

"Do you think he's… okay?"

"Just… give me a minute. Please."

David's jaw clenched. He swallowed hard, but let Sojourner go with a nod.

She crossed the living room and the hallway, knocked gently on Sean's door, and slipped into the room. It was dark and Sean sat on the bed, staring out the window.

"I'm sorry, Mom." His breath hitched with emotion.

Sojourner sat on the bed. "I know."

"I didn't think it'd be so late and I—"

"You had sex with that girl."

Sean's eyes widened and he started shaking his head in denial.

"It wasn't a question, Sean."

He stopped moving. Sojourner sighed and folded her hands in her lap.

"This was inevitable, I suppose. I just didn't expect it to be this soon. And I hoped. I hoped it wouldn't be like this, that you'd continue the way your father and I expected."

Sean experienced the deepest embarrassment he'd ever felt. His stomach tumbled and he started to tremble. Everything felt wrong: the night, his room, the dark, his mother. *The entire world.* Dull and wrong. He tried to make sense of his mother's words, to parse what she was saying and he couldn't. He wished he were anywhere but here. He'd be at summer camp next week, and he knew the days between now and then were going to be unbearable.

Sojourner said, "Is she okay?"

It took Sean a moment to come back from his confusion and hear the question. The pit of unease spread from his stomach into his feet. "What do you mean?"

His mother stared at him, silhouetted in front of the window next to his bed. "I meant what I said."

Sean took a deep breath and said, "I think so. She was... upset, after."

Sojourner said nothing in return. The silence stretched to an uncomfortable length. Sean slumped, cradling his head. His mother rose from the bed, startling him.

"Whatever you're capable of is... a responsibility, Sean. We can't watch you every minute of the day. Don't do this again."

She left the room and Sean lay there with his spiraling thoughts. His mother's words made sense to him, of course, but they felt like a knife had spoken them, not the woman who helped raise him. It was a side of her that he'd never seen and heard tell of from his father, on occasion. He curled up and soon drifted to sleep, exhausted. He dreamed in a spectrum of flesh and rivers of gold.

The morning brought civility by distance. Sojourner prepared breakfast and retreated to the back porch.

David spent the morning on the phone. Sean knew they both needed time to themselves to process, but they'd never dealt with anything like this before. And neither had he. He took his breakfast into his room and closed the door.

Thoughts of Donna intruded as he chewed, barely tasting the food. Would she ever speak to him again? He didn't have her number, but he knew where she lived. Would she ever do… that… with him again? The big 'it' dominated his mind. The act had been sublime, a moment that unmoored him in time, a unique experience in his life, so far. It hadn't been like what he'd seen in porn magazines or the film reels a friend-of-a-friend's father kept hidden. Not like the awkward moments described in novels either. It was amazing, until the end, when he'd finished and produced some bizarre discharge from a fever dream. The time they'd spent together before that had been oddly blissful as well, as if he were in sync with someone for the first time in his life. All of that was over now, however, things were exactly the way he'd remembered them. Except for his angry parents.

"Sojourner!" David's voice boomed through the apartment. He called a second time, before she answered.

"What is it?"

"I have to meet with Rome and a few others."

"Is something wrong?" Sojourner's voice came closer.

"Rome's cousin, at City Hall? He's been arrested. We need to help."

"It's happening again."

The sounds of David preparing to leave stopped. He said, "No, not again, it wasn't a protest or organizing or anything. Okay? Look, he was doing us a favor, so we gotta have his back."

"A favor?"

"Yes, a favor. Looking into some things."

"Is this about the clicks on the phone?"

David sighed. "Yes."

"Again," she said.

"This is different."

"Just go."

David groaned. Sean could imagine his father slumping.

"Just… Be safe," she said.

"I will, love." David left.

Sean thought about his scheduled month at summer camp. It couldn't come soon enough.

It was a beautiful day outside, but Sean remained hidden in his room. It'd been two days since he'd come home late after sex with Donna. He still had no idea how to get in touch with her, to apologize, or something. Going to her home was certainly an option, but the thought of being confronted by her *and* her family brought out the coward in Sean. None of what happened made sense. It wasn't like some out-of-body experience. To the contrary, it all felt right. Until it didn't. But it wasn't normal and that terrified him. He wanted to talk to someone who might understand, but that wouldn't be anybody he knew.

All the windows were open and a mix of cool air and fresh scents from the trees blew in. His mother tapped on the ajar door and it swung open. She held a regular white envelope.

"I need you to do me a favor and you need to get some fresh air. You've been cooped up too long."

Sean raised his eyebrows at her.

Sojourner stepped further into the room and held out the envelope. "This is for your grandmother. Your father hasn't had a moment to go by the home to drop this off. All you have to do is hand it over at the desk."

A few responses passed through Sean's mind. He wanted to ask why she couldn't do it. He wanted to complain that the home was all the way in the Roxbury. He wanted to say he was tired. None of that passed his lips. Instead, he took the envelope and said, "Sure thing, Mom."

"Thank you." And she left his room without another word or a smile.

Sean sighed and pulled his sneakers on before heading to the basement for his bike. He got the ten-speed out through the hatch, closed the steel doors, and made his way to the street. Cycling always felt like freedom. As fun as winter could be, not being able to ride his bike nagged. The hum of the rubber wheels on asphalt and the gentle clicking were soothing. As noisy as the city could be, all sounds were fleeting as he pedaled onto Morton and followed it across Blue Hill Ave. Taking the grand avenue all the way to Roxbury made sense in a car, but he could cut through Franklin Park on his bike. The park was the nice part of the ride, the streets were the challenging part. Vehicle drivers never seemed to care whether he lived or died when he was riding. Dodging potholes and parked cars opening their doors could be harrowing. He expertly navigated both streets and sidewalks. The breeze and physical effort lifted his spirits. By the time he was cruising downhill towards the park, racing along with cars on what felt like a highway, the doldrums of the previous two days were behind him.

One of the ancillary entrances to the park came hurtling up. It was blocked by massive concrete barriers that would keep any car from entering. He zipped between the blocks thinking of the first time he'd come this way. His father had shown him and it felt like they'd ridden so far and he was excited. At the time, he was on a purple, single-speed, fixed-gear bike. It had a fat rear tire with white walls and a sparkling, plastic banana seat. The handlebars were tall, like a chopper's, and from the grips flowed purple and white streamers. They'd come through here to ride "dead man's curve," a long, steep sidewalk that nearly hairpinned at the bottom before angling uphill. He'd never ridden that fast before on such a narrow path and he'd failed to check his speed by engaging the coaster brake. He panicked and sailed straight into the brush at the bottom before hitting the stone wall. A few scrapes, a few tears, some consolation, and some time later, Sean's father untangled his son's bike from the brush and they'd pedaled on.

This time was different. Sean tapped both his front and rear brakes, anticipating the sandy buildup at the bottom. His rear tire skidded through the curve and he used the momentum to sail halfway up the hill before needing to pedal again. His heart raced and he grinned, standing up and pushing through the steep incline. On the other side, a wider asphalt road awaited. It wound through the wooded area and he could mostly glide up and down the gentle hills.

He sat up, riding with no hands and spotted a figure on a boulder, well off the road. Low-lying brush and sparse trees separated the rock and the road. As he got closer, he could tell it was a young woman, but not much else. Color cascaded from her and spilled down the rock. The streaming colors faded at the edges into a fog of cotton-like whiteness and dissipated.

Sean cruised to a stop, staring. He could tell by the angle of her head that she was looking at him, but all of her details were lost in the kaleidoscope she appeared to be drenched in. He could feel his heart banging in his chest and wondered if it was the bike ride or something else. He waved. She waved back.

The decision was made before he was even aware of it. Sean dismounted from his bike and walked it through the low-lying brush. When he was within earshot, Sean called out.

"Hi, there."

"Hey," she said.

"Do you spend much time on rocks or just this one?"

She made a sound of mild amusement and said, "Just this one. Why?"

Sean grinned. At this distance, he could see more of her features. She was slim, almost skinny, with none of the usual neighborhood curves. Still, she was attractive, clearly a few years older than him, and smiling. He thought back to the moment he met Donna. The experience felt the same, he could do no wrong. Confidence emanated from him in a cloud of sparkling motes. He looked at his hands and rubbed his fingers together, exploring the tactile sensation of the effect. The motes touched the edges of the cascading pigments flowing from the woman on the rock. Where they collided, the bits surged upriver.

This isn't right, Sean thought, *but it feels…* He relaxed and more of the particles poured out of him. "I just wanted to be sure you were okay," he said and turned the handlebars of his bike, pointing it back to the road.

Sweat cooled on his forehead as his heart slowed down to a manageable beat. His thoughts became something he recognized.

"That's sweet, thanks," she said.

Before looking away, he said, "You're welcome. Bye."

They met over coffee at Brothers Diner. Rome, Teddy, and Peach were already seated at their usual table. David hustled in, saw that he was last, and grabbed coffees at the counter. All of them took it black, Teddy was the only one who added sugar.

Peach wasted no time, after greetings. "Rome told us what happened, why didn't you call us?"

David took a scant sip of his coffee and met Peach's light-brown eyes. She wore a silken headscarf that held her afro back from her face and matched her brightly colored dress. "It wasn't nothin' until it became something."

Teddy just shook his head. It was what he did when processing, a man of few words. They'd called him "Tank" for years until he'd put an end to it, not wanting a nickname associated with war. Rome appeared tense and reserved, nowhere near his gregarious self. This was the first time they'd met like this since they'd dissolved the BDP, years before.

Peach gave him a look that spoke volumes: disappointment, frustration, resignation, and a bit of encouragement. Black women had been communicating like that for years as they'd driven most of the civil rights movement. The BDP had been no different than most other progressive Black organizations. As much as the

BDP was considered at the same level as the Black Panther Party, no one else did it like they did.

David ran one hand over his hair and said, "I don't want to mix it up with the cops or Feds any more than any of y'all do. I just… I wanted to know if we were dealing with something or not."

"We still don't know," Rome said. "Cuz got pinched for stickin' his nose where it don't belong. We don't know if that's 'cause they was watchin' him or us or whatever. Thing is, it weren't no cop that pinched him, it was security in the building. They turned him over to the cops."

"So it ain't the cops," David said.

Teddy asked, "Think it might be a GIP still around?"

David shook his head. "I checked. I don't think so. If it weren't the cops or some damn informant, might could be the Feds. Rome? You ain't spoke to him yet, how you know what he got pinched for?"

"Friend in the department from back in the bush. Veterans are everywhere, man."

They all nodded. There were still some bonds that transcended race. How strong they were depended on the situation, however. This information wouldn't have cost Rome's veteran friend anything.

David took a deep breath and said, "Way I see it, this is on me. I'll handle Smitty's bail."

Peach reached over and put both of her hands on David's. "Way I see it, we'll all chip in for that." She glanced around the table and everyone nodded. "I'll get in touch with Oscar about representing Smitty to see this through. Best way to get at the feds is through legal means, so I'll ask about that too."

Peach's ex-husband had been one of the BDP's lawyers for years. Oscar was a fierce brother, David remembered, with a thick mustache and receding afro. He spoke with a growl, feared no white man, and favored tight, three-piece suits. "You think Oscar gonna be willing after…?" David tapped the empty space on Peach's left ring finger.

She sat back, smiling to herself. "Just 'cause we ain't married no more don't mean we don't talk."

David glanced at Rome.

Rome, sitting next to Peach, suppressed a grin and shrugged.

Teddy said, "He still wear them tight three-piece suits?

"That he does." Peach took a sip of coffee to hide her grin.

David said, "Our best bet is to try and flush something out into the open. I hope these inquiries might do just that, 'cause I do not want to be back on the radar like it was before."

Everyone at the table nodded again.

David sat back, considering how to protect himself and his family against this possible new problem.

Sean was nine the first time he went to summer camp. He remembered how hard he'd cried, believing with all his heart that he'd never see his parents again. He cried the second time, too, but not because he thought he'd never return, but because he knew the time at camp would be fleeting. This time, he felt the familiar twirling in his stomach and pressure behind his eyes as he bid his parents farewell while standing in the grass near Houghton's Pond. Lines of buses with numbers in the windows were lined up, end-to-end, waiting to move out.

Sean had stacked his bag in the appropriate spot, along with the others.

Kids from all over Boston were doing the same with their respective parents, all around them. Here and there, he saw some kids his age who still clung to "luvvies" from childhood: a small, stuffed animal; a ragged blanket; and one or two kids still had a thumb stuck in their mouths. He felt a pang of pity for them, kids could be cruel in unsupervised moments. Free time at camp could be brutal and free swim depended on being able to find a "buddy" to accompany you. No one wanted to be responsible for a kid still clinging to baby stuff. Being able to jump in the lake was the only respite from the sun during a hot summer.

Sojourner had been somewhat cold to Sean since "The Incident." Nothing else changed, but she didn't interact with him as often and instead chose to mostly observe him. It made him feel strange, more often than not, but at least she hadn't addressed him as royalty for several days.

"Goodbye, my prince," Sojourner said, looking wistful. "You've grown… too much." She hugged him.

Sean clenched his teeth and David chuckled. "You'll never outgrow that, Son, get used to it. Own it before it owns you." David pulled his son into a tight embrace. "Be smart, young man." He looked Sean in the eye.

"I will, Dad."

"And remember," Sojourner said.

"Remember what, Mom?"

She glared at him. "You know what."

He gulped and nodded.

Sojourner gathered him up and held him long enough to remind him that she loved him.

Men and women with clipboards began calling out

bus numbers and instructions. Boys and girls rode separate buses. It was time to go. Sean looked around the idyllic corner of the Blue Hills Reservation and, for a moment, the colors of summer danced. The most diverse set of kids he ever got to see rushed here and there. For one syrupy moment, he met the eyes of a girl wearing a pink top and jean shorts. Tight and shiny black curls covered her head and shoulders. The moment ended as quickly as it started. She faded into the crowd and he waved to his parents as he jogged to the bus.

The counselors checked off names and double-checked that everyone was who they were and where they were supposed to be before giving the okay for the busses to pull out.

Nervous, noisy, and excited, everyone waved and called out to their parents as each bus left the lot. For a moment, Sean wasn't the only one who couldn't hold back a tear or two. But only for a moment. It wasn't fear that drove his regret, this time.

Then they all fell into familiar patterns, reconnecting with camp friends and counselors. There was singing—the worst part, stupid camp songs—but they felt good, familiar. It wasn't the singing of the songs that was fun. The noise didn't die down until they were about to leave New Hampshire, heading for Maine. It was a three-hour ride, but it had felt like an entire day the first time Sean took the bus.

Within one week, Sean was fully acclimated to the rhythms of camp: breakfast, activities, free time, snacks, free swim after swim testing. The next few days were the organization's "Olympics" where all the campers mingled.

Boys and girls of all ages competed in established

Olympic sports and other outdoor activities. The younger the kids, the goofier the competition. Sack and egg race relays weren't his thing anymore. Now they had soccer, track, and archery—the last being his favorite. It was something he'd taken an interest in that was seemingly nonexistent in his neighborhood. Basketball, football, and occasionally baseball were the only sports anyone engaged in back home.

The day started with archery and it was a co-mingled competition. Being a somewhat slow process bogged down by safety measures meant that campers could talk. There were four targets available and a long line of kids waiting. Now that he was one of the older boys, he understood the attention they paid to the girls.

Rafael, a boy who lived somewhere in the same neighborhood as Sean did, asked him, "Yo, you talk to any of the girls yet?" He was Puerto Rican with a boxy head of curly hair, crooked teeth, and rapid-fire verbal delivery. He also started every sentence with 'Hey' or 'Yo' and it was a feature of any cajoling impression of him. When someone took it on, it was to shut him up.

"No, not yet."

Kevin said, "Not yet?"

Kevin was one of the larger kids, blustery and soft around the middle. Dark skin meant he only got darker as the summer wore on and he took some trash for it. Push him too far, however, and he'd come for you. His size and attitude meant he was to be respected. Sean was glad Kevin lived on the far side of Roxbury, well away from his neighborhood.

Sean had learned years ago to recognize the different levels of aggression coming off of people in the 'hood. He wasn't being threatened, but mildly challenged, and he'd best answer before the matter got out of hand.

"That's right, not yet. What? You slip out at night and canoe around the lake to have a word?"

Some of the boys took that as a sleight on Kevin's weight—not at all what Sean intended—and they chuckled about it. It did not help matters that Kevin was a poor swimmer and to see his fear when they were in or on the water was a sight.

"Bitches be on these shorts," Kevin huffed.

"Hey, Kevin, watch your mouth or you're out!" Tyler shouted. He was one of the lead counselors, a lean, blond man wearing aviator sunglasses. He had a horse-shoe mustache and the hair on top of his head was bleached almost white by the sun. Every summer he wore a tank top and jeans cut above the thigh with calf-high socks and canvas Cons. Everyone thought he was cool, like a character from TV.

Kevin said, "Sorry, Ty."

The counselor tipped his glasses down so everyone could see his blue eyes, then he turned his attention back to the games.

Rafael piped up. "Hey, Kevin ain't slippin' nowhere, 'specially in no canoe!"

Anger flitted across Kevin's face and his gaze stopped at Sean's face.

Sean shrugged and rolled his eyes before he said, "Y'all need to shut up. Ain't none of us spoke to the girls yet. This could be our only chance if we don't get more free time later."

The targeted comment landed and its delivery served to defuse Kevin's temper. The larger boy waved the whole thing off.

Rafael grinned and moved closer to Sean. "Yo, I bet you got your eye on someone. Who is it?"

Sean sighed and said, "I dunno. I only know a couple

of their names. I, uh, did see a girl with a pink top when we got on the buses to come here. Long, curly black hair?"

"Yooooo-oh, shoot, you mean Lluvia?"

The way Rafael said her name sounded like beauty to Sean's ears. The line shuffled forward, forcing everyone to realign. Sean caught a glimpse of Lluvia.

"You know her?" Sean asked Rafael.

"Yo, she live in my neighborhood, man, she Puerto Rican-fine and all that, bro, you don't stand a chance wit dat!"

Sean glanced over, making sure Lluvia wasn't looking in their direction. Then he took a good look. Every now and then, he could catch a glimpse of her profile as she chatted with the girls around her. He leaned out and counted the boys in front of him. Then he counted the girls in her line. If he wanted to be next to her, he'd have to navigate forward by three bodies. He had nothing to trade for the position. Sojourner wouldn't be sending brownies for another week and a half. Not everyone enjoyed comics the way he did. The only other item of value at camp was the "bug" juice the counselors served at the end of the day after group events. He could see the big orange jugs on the sidelines, condensation dripping down their sides. They were juice concentrates on plenty of ice and it was rationed tightly. It got the nickname for the occasional bug that died floating in the nectar. Besides the sporadic dessert after dinner, it was the only sweet available.

Sean turned to the boy in front of him. "Hey, Kev."

"What?"

"Lemme trade places with you."

"What the hell for?"

Tyler leaned out from the front of the line with his arms spread wide and eyes on Kevin.

Kevin mouthed, 'sorry' and tapped his forehead, in response.

"Look, man," Sean said, I just need to move up a few places. Please?"

"Hey, hey, heeeey, our boy here wanna talk to Lluvia," Rafael said.

Kevin sucked his teeth and said, "Naw, man."

"I'll give you my bug juice after this."

"No."

"My dessert then. Your choice."

That got Kevin's attention. "You mean whenever I say, you'll gimme your dessert?"

"Yeah. One time."

"Three times, chump."

Sean glanced at Lluvia's back. Her shiny black curls bounced when she laughed. She wore a bright yellow top interrupted only by her hair ending between her shoulder blades. The yellow bled like a halo of golden fire, streams peeling with the light breeze.

"Two. Now lemme by."

Kevin stepped to the side with an evil grin and waved Sean forward with a magnanimous flourish.

The next two boys took the bug juice deal. Sean stood parallel to Lluvia and stole furtive glances at the girl standing several feet away. She nocked an arrow, took a breath, and let fly. The bolt pierced the bullseye. Two more shots to go.

Impressed, Sean said, "Nice shot."

Lluvia smiled at him.

Sean drew his arrow and sighted down the shaft. He breathed deeply, taking in the sharp scent of cut grass, soil, and pine all around them. The feathers on the arrow tickled his cheek and the green around the feet of the target flowed like an ocean. The colored rings on the battered canvas of the target flared and swirled counter to each other. A silver mist of air swirled around his head and peeled back a path from the tip of his arrow to its destination. He loosed and hit the bullseye.

"Took you long enough," Lluvia said and let fly her second arrow. It too found center.

Sean nodded and put another arrow in the center of the target.

Lluvia's eyebrows raised before she refocused on her final shot. The arrow flew true and joined the others in a cluster. Sean's third arrow landed just outside the center.

"Can't win 'em all, I guess," he said to Lluvia.

Tyler called out for a cease-fire and gave the all-clear. The shooters jogged down to the target to collect their arrows.

Lluvia replied, "Unless I'm shootin'."

Bright white highlights swirled in her curls, leaving a glowing trail, and bits of diamond flecks sparkled in her eyes. He couldn't clear his vision and, like before, all was right with the world. *He flowed.*

"I'm Sean. And you are?"

"Don't act like you don't know me. I saw you talkin' to Rafael."

"Rafael's not the keeper of your name."

She smiled at that. "Lluvia."

Her name, again, sounded like magic to his ears coming from a native Spanish speaker. No L sounds, no V sounds, all soft vowels and gentle consonants that gathered tight in his brain. He repeated her name without flaw.

"Not bad," she said, before they walked towards the back of their respective lines. "You speak Spanish?"

"Non. Je parle un peu français."

Lluvia laughed. "What?"

"I speak a little French. It's the only language I've ever taken. I should learn Spanish, though."

"Tu no hablas Español."

Sean grinned. "Correct."

"So, you know a little. I could teach you more."

Sean's knees almost buckled as he watched the colors flow from her skin, blending into the rolling grass and the damp earth. It swirled through the air around her dark, sparkling head of hair. She beamed, gold flecks and soft white light flowed hazy from her teeth and eyes, mingling with the tiny motes popping from his skin.

Sojourner's words cut through his mind: *Don't do this again, Sean.*

He took a deep breath to settle himself and all the frosted colors twirled up his nose to set his brain alight. He tried again, breathing in and out to let the feeling go.

"When would you do that?" He asked, his voice a little breathless.

Lluvia shrugged. "Whenever we got free time next."

Sean could've sworn his feet were hovering above the shorn tips of the grass.

The next time turned out to be the end of the week. Being among the oldest campers, free time allowed them to wander the campgrounds a bit. The air had cooled, the sky darkened, and the inevitable patter of rain drove two groups of boys and girls to a barn on the edge of the campground, near the lake. They could see the mess hall through the wide open barn doors on one end and the lake through the doorway at the other.

Sean felt warm and giddy. The boys in his cabin, egged on by Rafael, had been stunned and effusive in their praise that he'd "pulled" Lluvia. Embarrassed, he denied the vulgar intent of the slang and tried his best to calm the cabin down.

Now, as he stood with Lluvia, the world, despite the drab gray atmosphere, appeared as a swirling smear of colors, thick and pure paints poured over everything. A sweet and pleasant scent hung in the air. As much as he desired the flow of scents and colors and sounds around Lluvia, he denied it, determined to let his experience be his own and not imposed on her.

Lluvia had won the gold arrow for her archery, and Sean the silver. Neither of them remembered who'd gotten bronze. They chatted with each other, mostly, for nearly an hour, giving only a cursory performance of being with their friend groups. With their free time fast coming to an end, Lluvia took Sean's hand and drew him quietly around back.

They stood close, underneath the overhang, out of the rain.

"Are you going to teach me some Spanish now?" Sean asked.

"Something like that," Lluvia answered, sliding one hand to the back of his neck and giving a gentle tug.

He traced her waist to the small of her back with his hands and leaned in. Tendrils of golden threads stitched them together. He inhaled her breath, a rainbow of colors spilling from between her slightly parted lips. He could smell the gold bleeding from her skin, hear the rush of cascading water her hair reminded him of. The threads tingled in all the right and wrong places. Sean struggled not to drown in her. Their eyes met and he tumbled anyway. Their lips pressed together briefly before parting to allow their tongues to entangle. The moment, he was sure, would never pass from his memory.

There was a flash of purple light akin to a lightbulb ending its life.

And then blackness.

Sean awoke in the camp's infirmary. Sweat pooled under his back and his skin itched.

"Oh, there you are!" The nurse hovered over him, a cold compress in one hand and a cup in the other hand. She was heavyset with short curly hair and wore a white, one-piece uniform. Her cheeks were bright red and glowed when she smiled.

Sean tried to speak, but she handed him the cup. It was juice concentrate, incredibly sweet.

"Drink up, you'll feel better. Tyler is bringing his car around to take you home."

"Home?" Sean said, thoughts of Lluvia running through his mind and other parts. "No, I don't want to go home yet."

"Dear, dear, dear," the nurse clucked, "No choice, I'm afraid, you have the Chickenpox and you are out of here. I'm so sorry, I know this is a great camp. Don't worry, we'll keep an eye on your friends." She winked and smiled.

Sullen and exhausted with fever, Sean met Tyler out front. He drove a wood-paneled wagon that chugged even while sitting in neutral, at a standstill.

"Hey, buddy," Tyler said, "you doing okay?"

"Uh, sure." Sean cradled the big, paper cup of juice.

"I'll get ya home in no time and yer mom and dad can take care of ya."

"Right, thanks." A wave of warmth driven by illness flowed through Sean and the world blurred.

Tyler patted Sean's knee and put the wagon in drive, then he flipped the radio knob and tuned in a station of rock and pop. Sean leaned his head against the window, thinking of Lluvia, how to find her again, and fell asleep as soon as they passed through the camp's main gates.

From Sean's perspective, the three-hour ride passed in an instant.

"Hey, kid," Tyler thumped Sean's knee. "We're here. I think."

Sean rubbed his eyes and blinked sleep from them. They were sitting at the top of his one-way street, Tyler's car chugging away. The sun had set and the streetlights glowed.

"This your street?"

"Uhm, yeah, we're here."

"You far down there? It's all random one-way streets here, how do I go around?"

"No, it's fine, don't bother. I can walk down."

"What? Are you sure?"

Sean opened the door, thinking it strange to see Tyler's face without mirrored sunglasses. "Yeah, yeah. Lemme get my bag." After collecting his bag from the back seat, Sean bid Tyler farewell and ambled down the hill. He didn't feel as hot anymore, but his skin still itched. It seemed like it took forever for the sound of Tyler's car to chug away toward Blue Hill Avenue. Thoughts of Lluvia didn't fade, though, he couldn't get her out of his mind. The possibility of getting it right, the draw he felt to her. It had been the same with Donna and the girl on the rock.

No, it was different this time, he told himself and wondered if every man thought like this, if every man had these experiences. The colors, the sounds, the tastes, the impossible harmony in two bodies coming together. With Lluvia, he felt wild and passionate, but in control. *Mostly*. Now that he was aware of the effects, he felt more in control. But that wasn't true, was it? He'd passed out while kissing a girl. There couldn't possibly be a way to live that down. It was because of the illness and not her, he told himself over and over. He'd never tell his friends, of that he was certain. Word would get out, though, when motormouth Rafael came home.

Rafael. The boy would be his only shot at finding Lluvia. They rarely saw each other. He had no idea how to contact him. It was going to take some effort.

He rang the bell to his apartment and waited to be buzzed in. There'd been no need for him to take a key to Maine. He wondered if both his parents were home or which one was letting him in. The harsh buzz and click told him to push on the heavy door. He was careful not to let it slam, knowing how much his father hated the boom and the potential for damage. The flight of stairs seemed longer than ever as Sean trudged up them, his bag over his shoulder. At the top, his mother waited.

Sojourner put her hands on either side of her son's face and took a deep breath while looking into his eyes. "Welcome home, my prince," she said, and kissed him gently on the forehead. "You have a fever. Come on, take a bath and…" She hesitated, wringing her fingers together. "Take a bath and we'll get you settled."

"Is Dad home?"

"No," was all she said.

Sean bathed. There were itchy bumps all over him. He felt hot and gross, even after the cooling shower. He slipped on pajama shorts and peered in the mirror. There were bumps on his face, his chest, all over his body. He looked more closely at the white-capped swells and caught a glimpse behind his own eyes. His brown irises swam with tiny flecks of light as if a storm brewed behind stained glass. He took one shaky breath and went to his bedroom. His mother waited there with a jar of ointment.

Sean sat on the bed. They both had one knee up and faced each other.

"Let me have a look at you." Sojourner reached for his face and looked closely.

Sean wondered what she was seeing, sitting so still and staring. It was difficult to look into one's eyes, to know oneself in that way. Sean had struggled to see in the mirror and wondered if his mother would find anything. He twitched when she broke contact and turned his head from side to side. She asked him to turn around. He did as he was told. She smeared cool calamine lotion on his back and shoulders.

"I hope that helps. Here." She handed the jar to him. "Put that on the rest of your… bumps, you should be able to reach the rest. And don't scratch. Then put your t-shirt on so the bed doesn't get ruined. You'll need to wash that off in the morning. Are you hungry?"

"No, I'm okay." He smeared the lotion wherever he felt an itch.

"Okay then. I love you, get a good night's rest." She kissed his cheek as he lay back in the bed.

"Good night, Mom."

"Good night, my prince," she said, a tightness in her voice.

Before she could cross the threshold, Sean called to her. "Mom?"

Sojourner stiffened and turned. "Yes, sweetheart?"

"What's going on with me, do you know?"

She went very still, not a breath, not a blink. The seconds seemed to drag on before Sojourner appeared to breathe again and she said, "Puberty. Chickenpox," without meeting Sean's eyes.

Part Seven: Escalation

On the fifth night of his illness, Sean awoke with a fever. Sweating, he threw his covers off and wiped his brow with a washcloth his mother had placed near the bed. He stared at the dark ceiling, watching colors swirl in the dark and hearing faint voices. He peered into the green glow of the clock on his nightstand. 12:43 A.M. The afterimage of the numbers floated around the room as he looked around and listened. He wasn't sure if it had been his parents or the fever that had awoken him. He could barely hear his parents. He focused, ignoring the sounds his own body made, the whooshing of his breath, the thump of his pulse. Then he cycled through the creaks of the house, the electricity coursing through appliances, water in the pipes, the settling of stone and wood.

"Are you sure?" Sojourner asked.

"No, I'm not," David answered. "I just wanted you to know what I suspect, so if you see anything—"

"If I see anything?"

"Yes. What?"

"Why is all this happening now, David? Why now? All this… tension and then Sean being sent home from camp…"

"Hang on, Sojourner, you promised, you said there'd be no side effects, that everything would be as it should be."

"I know what I said."

"Then what are you saying now? Sean has chicken-pox. That's normal. Why are you so worried about that? What is it? Are you not telling me something?"

The urgency in his father's hushed voice concerned Sean. He listened more closely, hearing a rush of air and gentle crunching. The screech of a doorknob twisting and the closing of a door made him jump. He didn't understand why it'd been so loud. He could still hear his parents, despite the closed door.

"Sean is our child, David, he—"

"I know, Soj, but—"

"He's as much a part of me as you, David—"

"'What in God's name is that supposed to mean?"

"A boy going through puberty."

David snorted. "You're telling me what?"

"He's fine. I don't see anything to worry about. Please, I… I promise I'll tell you if I notice something else, if I know it's definitive. As soon as I *know*. Please…"

"Okay, okay…"

"Now tell me what you're thinking is going on otherwise?"

Sean heard his father sigh and the awful creak of his parents' bed as someone shifted their weight. Sweat dribbled down his temple and fatigue pulled at his eyes.

"If we're being watched, it ain't anything formal. None of my contacts—or my contacts' contacts—or any of the other digging I've done indicate anything. Still, we have to keep our eyes open. Damn it, my paranoia is what got Rome's cousin in trouble."

"You may have asked him for help, but he had to make his own decision about how far to go."

David took a deep breath. "You know that's not how it works, Soj, you *should* know that by now."

"David."

"I'm sorry, Soj, I'm sorry…"

With his mother's stern response and his father's remorse, Sean drifted, bright lights swirled behind his closed eyes and he slipped into dreams. Down a twisting, liquid atmosphere, through sleek tunnels of ice, and into massive caverns. Indistinct forms flowed from cave-wall flowstones, like mercury and molten granite. Sean struggled to understand the sounds he was hearing—no, not *hearing*. He *felt* them, could feel sound ripple across his undefined skin in this strange place. He slid across a golden surface flecked with diamonds and silver, gliding until he hit an uphill curve. Rolling to look behind him, he saw that he was on a vast expanse of flesh. The gigantic nude form of a girl spread beneath him. He peered upward, past soft mounds into the face of Lluvia, then he tipped backward and sunk into boiling darkness.

Sean awoke to the smell of bacon and his skin felt cooler than it had in days. Some of the bumps still itched, however, and he squirmed in the bed, resisting the urge to scratch. His mother hummed "Wayfaring Stranger," a tune from Noel Pointer's *Phantazia* album. That was one of the records his parents listened to that Sean liked, but he was loathe to admit it. Looking at the clock, he realized how late in the morning it was. After such a strange night, he'd slept later than usual. His father was definitely at work already. Thinking back, he could hardly discern what had been real or a hallucination. He was sure of Lluvia, however, remembering that part of the dream brought a quiver to his stomach that wasn't hunger.

My behavior is the problem, Sean thought. *No, that's not right.* He sat up and knew there was some truth needling at the edge of his mind. *My choices—* "No," he said to himself and looked at the stack of comics on his desk. "I can't—what if I'm doing something to girls?" He recalled the spiral of his senses, how his inhibitions had been lowered almost as if by magic. The way things flowed from him to them and back. From him. To them. Like they were targets. *I made progress with Lluvia,* he thought. *I can control myself or whatever this is, I can control my own actions.*

The final thought felt good to him, clean somehow. Correct. Sean resolved to keep the conclusion top of mind.

Dishes clattered in the kitchen and he heard his mother's footsteps coming his direction.

"Good morning, my prince. How are you feeling?"

Sean eyed the plate she was carrying. It looked like a treat that only made appearances during times of illness: bacon and jam on toast.

"Hi, Mom. I feel much better today."

Sojourner handed him the plate and a napkin. With her hands free, she touched his forehead and back. "Fever's gone. Still itchy?"

Sean flipped the slices of toast together to form a sandwich and took a bite. Around a mouthful of sweet jam and salty meat, Sean said, "Only a little. Dad's not home, is he?"

"No, he left early to take the bus."

"Oh."

"More lotion?"

Sean shook his head, *No*, and focused on devouring the sandwich.

"Hm," Sojourner appraised her son. "Appetite's back." She smiled, peering into his eyes.

Sean smiled back, happy to see a crack in his mother's stoic façade. All the tension from before leaked away.

Then she cried. Not heaving sobs or signs of immeasurable pain. Sean noticed the crease between her eyes, the tilt of her brow. It happened through a sorrowful smile, like mourning a future that had yet to be.

"Mom," he said as softly as he could manage, unsure what to do or how to behave in a situation like this. "What's wrong?"

"Nothing, my prince." She took a deep breath and said, "It just hurts me to see you like this."

"I'm okay, Mom."

She nodded.

"Can I have another sandwich?"

Sojourner chuckled and said, "No. Eat a banana or something. Bacon isn't cheap."

As the morning wore on, Sean continued to feel renewed. He ambled into the bathroom for a shower. It always took several minutes for the hot water to reach the second floor. He couldn't imagine how much longer it took to get to the apartment above. As the water warmed, he stripped and looked into the mirror. The dried husks of the bumps were scattered all over his body. He sneered at the image in the mirror and once again regretted the invasion of pox on his penis. Only two bumps were there, but since he didn't want to exacerbate the damage, he'd remained chaste. Which was difficult, to say the least, considering the occasional unbidden thoughts of Lluvia. She was the only subject that pushed out his embarrassing and soured memories with Donna.

He looked into the mirror, staring at his pupils as the steam rose and clouded the mirror.

He jumped when his mother rapped on the door.

"Don't waste the hot water!"

"I'm not!"

Sean pulled back the curtain, stepped into the hot shower, and let the water peel away the last vestiges of fevered dreams and lustful thoughts.

David left work two hours earlier than usual. He'd arrived early in the morning, formulating a loose plan to satisfy his simmering paranoia. Taking public transportation meant being able to see everyone around him, who got off where, and what they were paying attention to. Considering his home neighborhood and riding a bus that white people colorfully referred to as "the jungle line," meant people who didn't belong would stand out. He'd already spent some time visiting neighbors and asking them to keep an eye out for anything unusual. The protests for Civil Rights weren't even a decade old, so they knew what he'd meant, and it took very little to fan the flame back to life.

To his relief, the commute home was uneventful with nothing out of place. It would only take a little more effort to put his concerns to sleep, allowing him to focus on his family again. The tension with Sojourner had been taking its toll, and being distant from his son for this was maddening. Not being as present as he needed to be, the past few weeks, with Sean beginning the transition from boy to man, caused him endless heartache.

David was glad to pull the cord one stop before his usual. Every pothole sent a sense-shattering crash through the bus and the endless rattle of change tumbling through the coin box still echoed in his ears. He crossed the wide and busy Blue Hill Avenue and cut through the neighborhood on the other side of Morton Street. He passed his street and crossed so that he had to backtrack home. His briefcase felt heavier than usual as he walked further than needed. The first pangs of ache coursed through his fingers and wrist. He cut across an empty plot and picked his way through the parking lot of the apartment building on the corner.

David peered through the hedges separating the lot from the abutting house and saw a white van across the street. There was a white man up the pole, working on the box, with short dark hair on the back of his head. He wore white coveralls and a yellow safety helmet. Beneath him, a similarly clothed, overweight compatriot looked up, offering colorful, encouraging commentary.

David stepped out onto the sidewalk and stopped, watching the men work on wires feeding his property. The van had something resembling the Bell System logo on its side. The men's clothing bore no insignia nor did they wear utility belts. A scuffing noise caught his attention. Another man wearing white coveralls and with dirty blond hair peeking from beneath his helmet walked quickly past him, stealing furtive glances at David, on the opposite side of the street.

Part Eight: An End in Sight

Right. Here we go, David thought, as he marched down the sidewalk and matched the man's pace. Adrenaline shot through his veins and he forgot the discomfort of carrying a briefcase as far as he did. The man across the street waved both arms and called to get his fellows' attention.

"Time to end shift!" He yelled up the street.

David kept his eyes alternating between all three men. The man at the top of the pole hurried to put away his equipment, dropped a bag to his fat friend at the bottom, and shimmied down the pole. David stopped at his front steps and put his briefcase down. Behind him, two of the van doors opened and slammed. He turned as the side door slid open and closed. He stepped into the street, eyes on the driver who steadfastly ignored him and turned over the engine. As he crossed, he noticed one of his neighbors looking down from their second-floor porch. A few others had gathered on porches or steps around them.

"Excuse me," David said, walking up to the window

and pinning the car into the parking spot. They'd have to run him over to leave.

"Oh, hey, how you doin'?" The driver glanced at David, keeping his head down and eyes beneath the visor of his helmet showing only a couple days growth of facial hair pockmarked with gray.

"Somethin' wrong with the phone lines here?" David asked, an unsheathed edge of sarcasm in his voice.

"Just routine. Excuse us, we have to get going. Can you step back?"

"Y'all from Ma Bell?"

The driver didn't answer, but his fat partner leaned across the center console. "That's what it says on the side of the fuckin' van. Right?"

The driver held a hand up to his partner and said, "Look around you, we're done here."

"Just sayin'," David took a short step to his right and pinched the corner of the rough-hewn decal on the side of the van.

Gears slammed into place as the driver put the vehicle in drive and hit the gas. The van lurched and David hopped back as it pulled out of the parking space. The vinyl between his fingers pulled easily off the side of the van.

"Just sayin', y'all's shit is peeling the fuck off!" David waved the bits of blue decal, taking note that the license plate on the vehicle was obscured. He cursed beneath his breath as the van topped the hill and screeched to the right.

"Yo, Dee!" David's immediate neighbor to the right called.

David met Willy's eyes. People on the street called him 'Dollar.' He had a white girlfriend named Carla who lived with him. Dollar called her 'CC.' David and

Sojourner had hosted CC on at least one occasion after one of the couple's epic fights had spilled into the street. Dollar, six-and-a-half feet of nervous energy in platform shoes and picked hair, aspired to be a pimp.

"The hell was that, man?"

David balled up the blue vinyl and said, "I really don't know, but it ain't good." He looked around the street at the neighbors who'd come out. Mr. Johnson was his immediate neighbor opposite Dollar. Mrs. Rowe was there with her twin boys. There was Isaac, Cheryl, Bobby…

Mr. Johnson said, "Ain't good? Who we worried 'bout now?"

David sighed and said, "Not sure, but it ain't who we might think. Might be something new, could be worse."

"Worse?" Dollar parroted. "We posse now?"

David clenched his jaw and glanced up to see Sean in the window. To Dollar he said, "Yeah. We posse now."

'Posse' meant grab a gun, if you had one.

Sean went to the window as soon as he heard his father's voice. He watched the scene below unfold. Saw his father confront the men unapologetically and stand up to them. Even when the van seemed it was about to strike him, he danced out of the way. Sean's heart skipped, watching his father in a situation like this. He had always felt that his father was indestructible and stronger than any other man. But he knew that wasn't true. He was old enough now to understand that his father was mortal and that white men could be a leading cause of mortality for Black men. But they were gone now and his father was coming inside. He turned from the window and startled to find his mother watching him.

The front door opened and she turned from the room before he could say anything.

"Soj—oh! There you are. Did you see those guys outside?"

"I did," Sojourner answered.

"How long were they there?"

"I don't know, maybe an hour. They weren't the telephone company, were they?"

"No. *Shit.*"

Sean walked into the hallway and asked, "What's going on, Dad?"

"What now?" Sojourner asked.

David paced a bit and put his briefcase down. "I'm not sure."

"Maybe they were here for someone else. A warrant?" Sojourner offered.

"I don't think so, they didn't act like cops at all."

Sojourner stiffened, understanding what it meant.

"Dad?"

"What is it, Sean?" David's answer was both louder and harsher than he'd intended.

Sean shrank. "I… I don't know what's going on? Why would anyone be watching us?"

In one stride, David embraced his son. He met Sojourner's eyes and said to Sean, "We are not free, Son, not yet. There's still work to be done."

Sojourner wrapped her arms around both of them.

***

Sojourner pulled away from her family and placed both of her hands over her heart. "I didn't think it would be… like this. I shouldn't have come, shouldn't have stayed." Her head shook back and forth as she turned and walked down the hallway.

They heard the door to the back porch open and close.

Sean, feeling a trill of panic, asked his father, "What'd Mom mean by that?"

David walked into the living room. "Come here, Son. Sit, listen."

Sean did as he was told.

David stripped off his sports coat and draped it on the back of his favorite chair before sitting down.

"A few years before I met your mother, I worked with BDP, the Black Defense Program—"

"I know—"

"Just listen. I was one of the Deacons of Research with the BDP and it was my job to gather, organize, and distribute information designed to uplift our people—"

His mother on his mind, Sean interrupted, "Dad, I know, but—"

"*Sean.*"

Sean settled down.

"It was the last part of my role that was the problem: distribution. Between my efforts, the disruption of extra-curricular schooling, and the organization's protest coordination with more vocal groups, we got unwanted attention. Significant unwanted attention. Your Uncle, Rome, was part of that effort, he was on the front lines in Vietnam and in America. The FBI's Counter Intelligence Program had us on their list and… it got ugly. We had more than one infiltrator from GIP—the Ghetto Informant Program—can you believe they actually called it that shit?

Anyway, what we did wasn't a secret or anything. Just

education and intellectual support whenever requested. We was like the Black Panthers but only focused on self-affirmation and political savvy. Again, it was that last part that was the problem with the FBI. See, they don't want us to be autonomous or equals. They want a servile class, an easily identifiable group without ambition or self-interest. That was the atmosphere I met your mother under. And, look, if 'they' is too confusing, I'm talking about white people, Sean."

Sean offered a nervous smile. "I know, Dad." To him, his father gave off the shivering tension of a longbow drawn and aimed.

"To be clear, Sean: *you cannot trust white people*. They think they are the be-all and end-all of *everything* in America. They believe their hands and their hands *alone* built this country and that they alone deserve the fruits of that imagined labor. You push hard enough and they are willing to kill you to maintain that illusion. That is what was happening in front of our house tonight, *that* is what's going on at all times and you must be ready *at all times* to deal with it. Do you understand?"

Sean nodded, knowing how little attention he paid to history books irritated his father. Black history before, after, and during the United States' existence was a vague shape in his mind. Sean's stomach churned, a hard ball of fear spinning and bouncing off his ribcage. Despite all of this, he wondered more than anything about the circumstances under which his father and mother met. The environment leading up to his birth had been so tumultuous. How could they make the decision to bring a child into this world?

And before the questions could cross his lips, his father said, "Okay, Son, that's it. I have to go talk to your mother now."

David patted his son's knee and left the room.

———

David cracked the door to the back hall and said, "Soj, you out there?"

She answered with a sigh.

David clenched his jaw and walked onto the porch. Sojourner stood facing the line of trees that bifurcated one street from the other. A light wind blew, causing the trees to make a shushing sound like the ocean's breath.

"We should have fought harder," she said, staring into the dwindling murk of twilight.

David shrugged and said, "That's always true."

Sojourner, arms crossed, glared at him. "No. I meant, to the death. We should have killed those who organized against our very existence."

"Sojourner…"

"I'd've supported that more fervently than King's doctrine. *That* passion would've made me feel more akin to the other women in the BDP. Organizing to kill would've made more sense to me than giving them the opportunity to kill us by inches. Death would have been better than this creeping progress. I shouldn't've stayed."

David blinked, unsure what to say. He licked his lips and struggled to draw an even breath. "Then why did you? For the cause? For… Sean?" He didn't think her face could become darker, angrier, and it surprised him. She turned her body to face him.

"You know damn well why."

If there were ever a moment that David thought Sojourner might strike him, it was now. She hesitated, though, then took a single long stride towards him. He didn't flinch. She embraced him. The hug was strong and definitive. David hugged her back, remembering why she stayed and what that had meant to him. He would fight for her, for Sean, to the death, if need be. He hoped this situation wasn't the case. However, even the creeping progress they'd lived through was better than death, in his reckoning.

David lowered his head into his wife's hair, breathing in her beguiling scent, so different than any of the other women he'd ever known. She pulled away after a few minutes.

David swayed and said, "Is Sean... okay? Is there something I need to know?"

"He... He should be fine. It's just puberty. I think." Tension laced her words and the stiffness was apparent in Sojourner's posture.

"Sojourner, c'mon. I'm a man, I was a boy once, I know what it's like and something's different with Sean. You told me there'd be no difference."

"There isn't. Not really. Not that I know of. But it's not science, David, it's new to me too. Our boy is as much as I expected and so much I didn't."

David waited for her to say more, something reassuring or explanatory. She remained silent as dusk settled over the neighborhood and the whine of insects rose.

Part Nine: Not a Plan

Recovering from chickenpox was not how Sean expected to spend the end of summer. He'd missed the first day of school and even though he'd been symptom-free for twenty-four hours, his mother had insisted he stay home one more day. It was maddening and he was begging to leave the house by midday.

"C'mon, Mom, I haven't seen my friends for more than two weeks."

Sojourner knelt in front of the freezer, digging for something to go with dinner. "They're at school anyway, so you can't see them until later. And they'll probably have homework."

"Then can I go meet Dad after work?"

She actually smiled. Only the second time Sean had noticed, in the last few weeks. The first time had been when his pox faded.

"You want to go to that hole-under-the-tracks 'bookstore.'"

"It, uh, had occurred to me."

"You call your Dad, first?"

"Yup."

The freezer door thumped shut and she sighed. "Fine. If you leave in a couple of hours, you'll have time to browse and meet your dad."

Sean gave his mother the double-gun fingers and said, "Thanks, Mom!" For the next two hours, he hunted for something to read that he hadn't already reread more than twice or maybe a few clean pages within his sketchpads. Anything to distract from the passage of time and whatever anxiety he felt about his parents.

Strolling down the street, breathing in his first freedom in weeks, felt odd but relief flooded his heart. Getting anywhere in Boston took about an hour on public transit, so he hustled the four blocks to the bus stop. There weren't many people out in the neighborhood, with all the kids in school. Along the way, on the bus and train, he took in the smells, sounds, and sights of the city as if he'd never experienced them before. Asphalt and exhaust, dirt and concrete. The distinct scent of rubber in mats and seals on the bus, the harsh rattle of coins being processed in the fare box. The metallic scent the fare had left on his hands. The bang and rattle of bus windows from potholes. The roar of engines, the scent of oil and gas. Diesel and steel on the elevated platform and grease and plastic within the subway cars. The distinct smell of the trains' tunnels carried on bursts of warm air and the buzzing of power lines. Pigeons, discarded cans, the sound of a jet overhead. For the hundredth time, he wondered what it'd be like to fly and felt lighter than ever before. Lighter, not overwhelmed. It felt natural to him, more natural than before, and no different than whatever had passed as normal during the previous years of his life.

Beneath the elevated tracks, Washington Street

remained forever in shadow and occasional rain. Filth gathered in the darker patches where sunlight never penetrated and water pooled in hidden spaces above. The hodgepodge of retail and offices along the strip on the outskirts of downtown were old when Sean was born. The edges of everything looked ragged and worn.

Human, he thought.

Where people had lived and worked and worn down the world they'd built on top of the world that'd grown. It was past time to refresh everything in the city. Despite the decay and racism, this was home and he couldn't imagine living anywhere else.

The store remained unchanged, like most of the city. Behind the counter, as usual, stood the man with the thick Van Dyke. "Ain't seen you in a while," he said to Sean.

Sean said, "Nope."

They stared at each other for a few seconds, until Sean turned to the boxes of books and comics. He was anxious to get lost in the box of hidden treasures. Sliding into familiar habits, the things in his life that sparked personal joy. Simpler times, even.

In the comic bin, he found a worn copy of *The Incredible Hulk* fighting someone named Wolverine with claws on the backs of his hands, but he couldn't cut the Hulk's skin. The yellow suit looked odd too. And there was the Wendigo, looking like a white werewolf. This was a continuation of a story he had at home. Herb Trimpe drew a great Hulk, so he set it aside and dug further, finding an intriguing black-and-white comic about someone called Star-Lord. He found an *Iron Fist* and two issues of *Man-Thing*, but he left those in the bin since Fist had become boring and Man-Thing just too weird for his tastes. *The Uncanny X-Men* he kept along with two issues of *Luke Cage, Hero for Hire*. He found one copy of *The Defenders*, with Hulk, Sub-Mariner, and Dr. Strange. They were the oddest most overpowered team in Marvel's history and this issue featured Silver Surfer too. Even more ridiculously overpowered. Always a must-read comic.

"How was your summer?"

Sean popped his head up and looked around. The store was empty, the clerk was talking to him. A chasm of silent stoicism three years deep yawned between them. "Uh, good."

"Just good huh?" The man grinned.

Sean wasn't sure what to think of this. So he just said, "Yeah." However, the more he thought about what was happening, the more he realized that he'd never been alone in the store with the clerk.

"When I was your age, we spent most of our time chasin' girls. But here you are, your head in a box o' funny books!"

Sean grinned and held up a *Man-Thing* comic. "Not funny." He put the comic down. "And there's plenty of girls, they ain't goin' nowhere."

"'Zat right, li'l pimp man?"

Sean snorted. There was no way he was going to cop to that. "I'm doin' just fine, man. Why you wanna know?"

"Just talkin' is all. Kinda borin' sittin' here all day, sometimes."

Sean nodded. "Where you get all these books from, why the covers pulled off?"

"Ah," he shrugged, "it's complicated. But a discount's a discount, am I right?"

Sean's thoughts tumbled to Lluvia. He hadn't seen Rafael since camp or anyone who knew him. The boy was his only connection to Lluvia and it looked like that connection was never going to happen.

"There was this one girl, Lluvia, at summer camp…" The words left his mouth before he could think to stop them.

"Lluvia, huh? Shit, man, that's a beautiful name. She match up to her name?"

"I thought so."

"But you don't talk to her no more? How come?" The clerk leaned forward and joked, "You too nerdy for her?"

"No," Sean snorted. "I got sick, Chickenpox. They had to send me home and I have no idea where she lives or nothin.'"

"Oh, damn."

"Yeah," Sean said. He stared at nothing between them for a beat and said, "Yeah," once more.

Sean turned his attention to the box full of books. It was slower going, since all the covers had been removed. He found a collection of Isaac Asimov stories, an author he was familiar with. He was running out of time and couldn't make a decision on the rest, books with uncomfortable descriptions like *Demon Seed* by Dean Koontz or incomprehensible descriptions like *The Faceless Man* by Jack Vance.

At the counter, the clerk placed one hand on the stack and took a deep breath. "You shouldn't give up."

"Huh?"

"On this chick, Lluvia."

Sean sighed and said, "Why not?"

"'Only when it is dark enough can you see the stars.'"

Sean squinted and shook his head. "I… don't…"

"Dr. Martin Luther King, Jr."

"Okay."

The clerk sucked his teeth and made a comically frustrated sound. "Hope, young man, it's about hope."

"He was talking about oppression." Sean surprised himself by placing the reference. And in context, remembering the quote and the words around it.

"He was talking about the best in us coming out when it's darkest. I mean, his whole thing was about not giving up, right? Anyway, I always dug that line, ever since I heard it."

"*Heard* it? You were there?"

The clerk nodded. "I was volunteering for the Poor People's Campaign in Memphis. After that racist piece of shit assassinated Dr. King, I decided the South wasn't for me no more and here I am telling you to keep at it."

Sean appraised the man in an entirely new light.

"Maybe I'm a hypocrite, you know? But love—"

"—I never said I was in love."

"Love is the binding force of the universe, you can't help but be in it, chief. Anyway, enjoy the reading."

The clerk smiled, an arrangement of his face that Sean had never seen until today, and it was tinged with sadness. Then, like all the other times, Sean paid for his damaged bounty and left feeling dirty and poor, but rich with the weight of art. His father waited at the corner.

"Hey, Son." David hugged Sean with one arm, the other hand occupied by his briefcase. "Find anything good?"

Sean smiled, "A few things. It feels good to be out of the house."

"I bet, I bet." David craned his neck as he guided his son.

Sean noticed they were moving at a quicker-than-normal pace, that his father seemed wary, looking out for something.

"What's up, Dad?"

"Hm? Oh, Sean. It's just… I'm concerned about, y'know, what happened on our street the other day. It doesn't help to hide, but you can't be too careful. Y'know? The car's on the block around this corner. I just want to get home, is all, get on with our lives."

His father drew up short, pulling Sean back. David took a half step, putting his body between his boy and the two men in front of them.

Both were about six feet tall, the same height as David, but one was heavier around the middle. He wore a threadbare dark suit buttoned over his overflowing gut. Balding with a thick mustache and stained teeth, he grinned at David.

"Mr. Lenun? I'm Special Agent Schmidt and this is Special Agent Fowler."

Fowler was much leaner than his partner and wore a tan suit with a fat, poorly tied knot at his neck. At least two days of facial hair connected his mustache to thick sideburns. He held a bare ID with his smug face that said 'FBI' on it.

"We're gonna need you to answer some questions. If you'll come with us?"

David peered at the two men for less than a second before bending over and whispering in Sean's ear, "As soon as it happens, run."

Confused, Sean asked, "What?"

"Do what I tell you, Son." David drove his fist into the fat man's gut.

Sean flinched, shocked at the violence on display in front of him, perpetrated by his own father.

David pushed the gasping Schmidt into Fowler. He raked his son behind him, pushing the boy further down the sidewalk and yelled, "Run!"

Sean saw his father punch Fowler in the face and kick Schmidt in the balls, before he took flight. The grunting, shuffling sounds of a fight faded behind him. He ran. His only purpose was to follow his father's order. Before turning the corner, he looked back. Schmidt was on all fours, gasping at the sidewalk. The skinny man, his face red from the nose down, reached into his waistband for the handle of a pistol. David lunged at him.

There was a crack of sound, a man's scream, and Sean's feet moved of their own volition, taking him around the corner and down a side street, startling a few people leaving work. In his arms he clutched the paper bag of books and comics. He sprinted across the street to the right, running parallel to the elevated tracks a block away, and turned again, moving quickly through the slow traffic downtown. He turned one more time, the highway in his sight a few blocks further. Nothing looked familiar, he couldn't retrace his steps, sweat stung the crevices of his body. He stopped and crammed himself into a deep doorway, hiding from the late afternoon light.

Sean's heart thundered and he could feel the push and pull of the valves in his body drawing blood from head to foot. The sound of his breath whooshing through his lungs ebbed and flowed. He pushed further into the corner, willing his body to be small, begging for his father to be okay, to be bulletproof.

He pressed harder into the corner, the colors of the city swirling in his sight. Brick red, muddled gray asphalt, rusting iron, torn stickers, and haphazard graffiti. He felt a terrible fear and worry for his father and, most of all, he felt alone.

Time passed because it always did. Sean wasn't sure how long. Every minute felt like an hour. The light didn't appear to change much, however, so he assumed he hadn't been hiding for long. People passed by, but no one looked at him. No one showed any concern for the Black boy huddled in the corner.

"Sean?"

His father's voice, but the man himself was nowhere to be seen. He heard his name called again, but felt glued in place, unable to speak. David came into view, still carrying his briefcase. He was sweating and appeared rumpled, roughed up, but alive. No serious wounds. He was alive! David looked directly into the doorway, but saw nothing. He craned his neck and called Sean's name again.

The boy lurched from the doorway, dropping his bag and startling his father.

"Sean! Jesus Christ, boy, you scared the hell out of me!" He wrapped his arms around his son, the briefcase slapped Sean in the back. "Where were you?"

"I was right here, Dad."

"What?"

"Right there," Sean spun and pointed into the doorway, "right there in the corner."

"I looked and didn't see you at all."

"You're okay, that cop pulled a gun! I saw you jump at him and the gunshot and—"

"—Okay, okay, I'm okay, we're good. And those men weren't police." David adjusted his position so that he could look directly into Sean's eyes. "They were *not* policemen and they weren't FBI. I have seen the identification and badges of both enough to know the difference between pigs that work for the city and pigs that work for Hoover."

Sean trembled and David took him back into his arms.

"They weren't the same men at our house were they?"

The panic in Sean's voice broke David's heart. "No, these were different guys. But I bet they know each other. Look, Son, I don't know what's going on, but it's done now. Let's go home. Okay?"

"Okay, but… the gun, what happened?"

David stood up straight and rummaged in his briefcase. "I took it from that punk after he almost shot his partner." He held a short-barreled revolver. "And they not getting it back." David rubbed the flap of his coat all over the pistol before he looked over the edge of the sidewalk, found a sewer grate, and tossed the pistol in. Then he hugged his son again, his hand on the back of Sean's head. He spoke into Sean's hair. "Why the hell you didn't run to the car, boy?"

The car chugged along Blue Hill Avenue. They'd cut through Roxbury and Sean strained to see the zoo as they passed. Boring as it was, the sight was the most interesting thing between downtown and home.

David glanced at his son, thinking of what had just happened and what was probably in motion. It didn't matter who the men were, his family was in trouble. They were trying to collect him, again, and there was no telling who else might be on the list. That the men weren't part of any enforcement agency complicated matters considerably. Regardless, he had some decisions to make.

"Sean."

"Yeah, Dad?"

"When I met your mother, there was no bomb."

"There wasn't an explosion?"

"Oh," David sniffed, "there was definitely an explosion. I was the only one who saw what it was, though." He licked his lips and remained focused on the road in front of them. "Your mother… arrived that day."

"What? I don't… I don't understand."

"There was a portal, just a flash of light, the hint of a tube or tunnel or something and there she was. Apparently, it's how her people handle interstellar travel. It—"

Sean refused the information with his entire body. "That can't be—"

"Let me finish, Sean! This isn't easy."

Sean put his hands up and gulped one or two breaths while slowly nodding.

"She arrived in the middle of a march and it was pure chaos. The… the transport system wasn't supposed to arrive there, it wasn't supposed to arrive in a built-up area. It was a mistake; they were rushed when they sent her and there was a miscalculation. That explosion, your mother's arrival, it was the beginning of the end of the BDP."

They drove in silence for a few beats, only the sound of the engine and wheels on asphalt.

"She was wounded when she arrived. In the mess that followed, she healed right in front of me. It was… stunning. And it costs her something to be able to do that. She collapsed. Rome helped me move her and evade the cops. I wasn't sure what to do, but a hospital was out of the question. I convinced the BDP that she had moved from Canada on that unfortunate day. It took time after that, but we were able to integrate your mom into the movement."

"When did you, I dunno, start dating?"

David took a deep, cleansing breath. "The more time we spent together, the closer we got. It's as simple as that. I've kept her secret all this time."

"But why did she have to come here? You said it was a rush and that she arrived wounded."

"Yeah. Okay, look I'm going to—"

"This isn't the way home."

"I'm taking you to Rome's before I go and get your mother. We'll meet there. I don't know what's happening, but we need to *not* be where these people can find us. At least long enough to figure out what's going on."

David pulled up to the curb and turned to his son.

"Go inside, tell Rome what happened downtown, and wait for me and your mother to come back."

A cold streak of fear filled Sean's stomach again. He felt nauseous, sick with worry, his head spinning with new information. "But, Dad—"

"Do it now. Go. And Sean? I love you, Son. I'll be right back.

Sean sniffed. "Okay, Dad." He got out of the car and stepped onto the sidewalk. His father peeled away, driving with as much urgency as the city would allow. An urgent buzzing rattled his ears while watching his father disappear around a corner. His mind raced with urgent questions that had no apparent answers. What it all added up to was the anxiety of love and separation. The kind of painful fear only a child could summon.

Part Ten: Run Again

Sojourner rubbed at the gnarled edge of a puzzle piece with fine-grit sandpaper. It was a thick block of wood, covered in colorful decoupage and ink drawings. The jigsaw had struggled, near the end, its blade nearly spent, but she'd pushed on and the result was jagged edges.

She heard the foyer door slam and heavy steps pounding up the stairs. The door swung open and hit the wall. David filled the doorway.

"Soj! We have to go."

Everything about him felt like it had over a decade ago, during the height of the movement. He was tensed, his clothes dirty and torn.

"What happened?"

"Soj, please." He hustled past her with a brief touch and into their bedroom.

"Where's Sean?" She didn't move.

She could hear the sound of drawers opening and shutting, the closet door being thrust open, something with weight tossed onto the bed. With deliberate steps, she set aside her tools, stood, and walked into the bedroom. David glanced at her.

"Just take what we need. Here, you get your things, I'll get Sean's."

"David. Where is my Son?"

David stopped, confused. It took him a heartbeat to focus and change tracks. "He's with Rome. I don't know what's happening. Someone's after us."

"And?" Sojourner remained still, hands loosely clasped in front of her.

To David's eyes, it appeared as if his wife had fallen out of focus, like the edges of her shape blurred. "And I want my family to be somewhere else before they try again."

David slammed a pair of jeans into the bag he'd thrown onto the bed and rifled through another drawer.

"When did this happen?"

"Huh?"

Sojourner repeated herself slowly, "When. Did. This. Happen?"

"Shit, Soj! Downtown. Two guys pretending to be FBI. Same type of white dudes was here with the utility van the other day, they don't fit the roles they play. Tried to take me in front of Sean."

Sojourner took a deep breath while David shoved socks and underwear into the bag. He turned, ready to collect more clothes for Sean. Sojourner grabbed his face and held him there, a velvet vice, staring into his eyes.

"You're hurt."

"Only a little."

"Was Sean hurt?"

"God, no. I told him to run and I tussled with 'em enough that we could get away."

She held his face a moment longer, her eyes boring into his. "That's all?"

He could see the swirl of color behind her pupils, a bright line danced along the dark edges. "We got away, Soj, but they're still coming. I think these assholes are **COINTELPRO** leftovers, fools who think they still have the FBI at their back."

David leaned forward, Sojourner's hands slipped behind his head, and he kissed her. He let every memory of their time together, every moment of success and loss pour through him. She felt it, he didn't have to say it.

Outside, there was the screech of tires and someone started shouting.

"You want somethin' to drink, m'man, I got some Cokes?"

Sean, sitting at Rome's dinette table, dragged his tapping fingers across the yellowed formica. "Sure, yeah, thanks, Uncle Rome."

The paper bag of books and comics from earlier sat untouched beneath Sean's seat. He looked around Rome's small apartment: the threadbare furniture, a black and white television, a bookcase full of books, and a wall of photos. Wall-to-wall carpet put the cap on a library-like silence, but the faint smell of weed dispelled any notions. Sean wondered how much Rome knew. His father's revelations churned in his head and he struggled with the new information, wanting to talk to someone about it. As his eyes roamed the walls and shelves, one photo in particular caught Sean's eye as Rome set a glass of soda in front of him.

Sean mumbled thanks as he rose from his seat, eyes

on the photo. He pointed, drink in hand, at the image on the wall. "When was this one taken?"

Rome smiled and took a seat at the table, a rocks glass with one finger of a clear liquid inside. "That was round about the end of days for the BDP, just after one of our last meetings."

Sean's father, mother, and Rome—watchman's cap forever perched at an angle on his head—posed in a bright room. The trio were surrounded by plastic chairs and folding tables, in a broad, drop-ceiling room.

"Where?" Sean asked.

"That was at the Johnson Community Center, in the basement. After that it became a synagogue, and after that a church, and now it's just empty. But we used to meet there, sometime, when the organization was going full."

"You look so happy together. This would've been a bad time for y'all, but you look happy."

"We are friends, nephew. That sort of trumps everything else. Even after you been damn near blowed up."

"Was this around the time my parents met?"

Rome leaned back and took a deep breath before answering. "Naw. That picture was almost a year later."

Sean waited. He watched Rome and waited for him to fill the air with words.

Rome sighed and suppressed a smile. "Your pop didn't tell you how they met?"

Sean shrugged and said, "He told me they met at a protest that was bombed."

"Sounds about right. Your mom had come down from Canada the day before. Your dad didn't have time to introduce us before things went boom."

"So you didn't help him cover up her arrival or anything?"

Rome leaned forward and clasped his hands on top of the table. He bit his lip and watched Sean for a few seconds before responding. "Your dad told you that?"

Sean nodded, certain that Rome wasn't in on the truth.

"Well, that sounds about right too." Rome leaned back and put one arm over the back of his chair. "Not unusual at the time. We had certain people come and go in mysterious ways. Life was very different for Black folks, back then. It's better now, but…" Rome's words drifted off and he waved a hand to indicate everything at once.

Sean thought of his friends and what they might be doing now. He hadn't been able to see much of them since being sick and recovering. He'd much rather have been hanging around with them than this agonized waiting. "Can I use the phone?"

"Nope."

Stunned, Sean said nothing for several heartbeats. He took a sip of Coke, burped and asked, "Why not?"

"This just how we do, Sean, in situations like this. I don't think I'm bein' watched—these folks who *are not* FBI don't seem to entirely have their shit together—but that don't mean we don't gotta be careful. You dig?"

"Yeah." Sean took a deep breath and sighed before peeking through the curtains at the front window. The street below looked much the same as when he'd arrived. Nothing had changed.

Rome's apartment was inside a heavy brick building. In the silence, Sean could hear his own pulse. The tap of Rome's glass was incredibly loud, same as the phone's ringing.

Rome snatched the plastic yellow receiver from its nestling place in the cradle mounted to the wall. He said,

"Yo," and walked into the kitchen, stretching the long, coiled cord. He didn't say much, just 'yeah' and 'okay' a few times before slamming the device back into its cradle and confronting Sean.

"You stay here." Rome strode into his bedroom and started rummaging around.

"What? But…"

Rome came back into the living room, sunglasses and jacket on. He adjusted his shirt at the small of his back and shoved his wallet and keys from the counter into his pockets. "*Here*, Sean. You hear me? I'll be right back with your parents."

"Okay."

Rome opened the door and paused, peering at Sean over his sunglasses. "*Here*."

"*Okay*."

Sean stared at the street below until he saw Rome's green Pontiac roar out of the back lot, from the side of the building.

David hustled to the window, Sojourner at his side. A black car had screeched to a halt in front of their home. Another followed. And two more, both brown. From the first car, two white men leaped out, shouting at the others spilling from their cars. Some of the men were obviously armed, the others may have had pistols, it was difficult to see from the second-floor window. One of them pointed at David's home and yelled, "David Lenun, by the authority of the FBI, surrender yourself!"

David yelled back, "That's bullshit, you ain't FBI!"

"Hey, motherfuckers!"

The third voice was Dollar's. He sounded confident. Too confident.

"Oh, Soj," David said and made for the stairs.

Sojourner reached for her husband, sure she could stop him, but ultimately unwilling to do so. She followed at an unsure pace despite her past rhetoric advocating open conflict.

David skipped down the stairs, moving into action without a plan, without thought. As he burst onto his enclosed front porch, a shot rang out and all the men who'd just arrived ducked as one of them cried out and toppled.

Dollar stood on his porch, a joint dangling from his lips. He was the portrait of cool: shirtless, tight jeans, gigantic belt buckle, and holding a black .38 pistol. He looked like the proverbial poster for a fifty-cent movie. He was higher than clouds and waving the pistol with sharp snaps of his wrist.

"Get the fuck out here fo' I put down more o' you crackers!" Dollar shouted.

David called out to his neighbor, "Dollar, get down—"

The intruders opened fire. A hail of bullets chewed up the front of Dollar's triple-decker. He snapped like a paper doll in the wind as wildly fired rounds tore him to bits.

Once again, David found himself in motion without thinking. He rushed down his front stairs and crashed through the front gate. Across the street, Mr. Johnson leveled a long, black shotgun.

The word 'no' was on the tip of David's tongue when the blast ripped through the air and shattered one of the car's windows. Johnson racked another round and fired again. Birdshot rang off the cars and one of the men went down screaming, streams of blood pouring between his fingers, holding his pellet-struck head.

The group of white men turned their sights on the old man. For his part, Mr. Johnson had the wherewithal to look shocked at the entire affair.

David careened into the nearest shooter as the group started firing again. He was close and punching hard. The men had to refocus their efforts lest they shoot each other. He fought like a maniac, hitting whatever came into reach. They fought back, using handguns as cudgels. David felt no pain, only the excavated rage buried years before.

The neighbors poured from their porches and joined the melee. The entire street descended into chaos, a boiling mix of anger and resentment. More glass shattered, people fell to the ground, some didn't rise.

David stumbled more than once, managing to catch himself on a car or another person in the melee. One of the men pirouetted into him and David threw him to the ground, stomping hard with his heel. He heard Sojourner'svoice yelling his name. It sounded like she was miles away, yelling through cotton. A sharp blow to the back of his head sent him into the street on his hands and knees. He felt three searing blows to his back and his limbs gave out. He couldn't breathe anymore, couldn't move. From the twisted angle, lying in the road between cars, he could see the reflections of the fight around him. The man who'd shot him appeared to be twisting, his head spinning. Sojourner's face flashed into view as she dealt with her husband's killer, fingers flashing red, her face an unrecognizable rictus of malice. She dropped the man to the asphalt in a heap. His body faced David and he could see through the wash of blood over the man that his eyes were blank and frozen in death.

Sojourner gathered David into her arms and sobbed, knowing what came next. She could see the light swimming in her husband's eyes swirling away. David wanted to hug her back, to kiss her, to tell her he loved her and that he'd be fine. Over her shoulder, Rome appeared.

As soon as he saw his friend's face, Rome knew that he was too late. But not for Sojourner. He pulled at her shoulder, unable to move the woman.

David struggled to hear. The sounds of the fight faded and he wondered if it was finally over. He could see Rome's panicked face and his lips moving as he struggled to get Sojourner's attention, to get her to move.

David worked his mouth over and over, but Sojourner couldn't see it. He couldn't form a sentence, couldn't muster the strength to draw air.

With a final effort, David managed to say, "Go."

And nothing more.

Sean looked at the clock. The wait felt like hours, but it had only been forty minutes or so. The last bits of ice in his glass collapsed, the tinkle of it loud in the apartment. A pool of water had spread beneath the icy container, so he put it in the sink and grabbed a towel from the kitchen to mop up.

He heard voices in the hallway, urgent and coming up the stairs fast. He didn't know what to do and stood listening as the lock turned and the door swung open. His mother rushed into the room and it was several seconds before Sean processed that she had blood on her hands and face. Rome stood behind her, a wild look on his sweat-slicked face. He snatched the watch cap off his head and ran his fingers across his forehead and through his coarse hair.

Sojourner locked eyes with her son and hesitated. Her eyes brimmed with moisture and she glanced at her hands.

"Mom?"

"Wait," she answered and breezed past Sean, heading for the kitchen.

Breathless, Sean watched as his mother washed blood from her hands. He didn't see Rome cross the room and stiffened when Rome gathered him into a bear hug. "I'm sorry, Sean," Rome whispered in his ear. "We have to get moving."

Sean stumbled when Rome rushed away in a gust of air.

"Mom?" Sean said, his throat tight and his words pouring out in an agonizing stream. "Whose blood is that? Where's Dad?"

Sojourner slid over to her son and gathered him in her arms. She squeezed, and buried her face in his hair. "My prince, my prince, my prince…" She repeated the phrase a few more times before Sean asked again where his father was.

Sojourner pushed Sean out to arms' length and held him there. His mother's strength surprised him.

Rome came running from the back of the apartment and looked out the front windows. "We have to go," he said. "Now."

Through his shock, Sean could see something unrecognizable had settled over Rome. The man he'd known as his uncle for his entire life had lost all the laid-back energy and replaced it with a coldness. His eyes were still covered by reflective shades and the ever-present watch cap remained in place on his head.

The room tipped and spun. Sean could barely make out his mother in a run of color and sound that rushed his ears. His knees buckled.

"Sean, stay steady." Sojourner said, holding her son up by his biceps. "Let's go." Was she speaking to Sean or Rome? He couldn't tell as they hustled from the apartment with Rome in the lead.

They rounded the first flight of stairs and Rome paused to glance out the small window on the landing. "They're here. Keep moving, that way."

They traversed the long hallway on the second floor to the stairs in the rear. Sojourner's hand at Sean's back remained a solid and welcome guide. Outside, through the wooden fence, Sean could see some of the men who'd arrived. They milled frantically, trying to decide how to enter the building. Sojourner pushed Sean into the back seat and sat in the front. Rome paused, halfway into the driver's seat, and stared ahead at the men.

"Fuck it," he said and dropped in, slamming the door. He gunned the engine to life and the car lurched forward when he slammed it into gear.

Sojourner braced one hand on the dash and said, "Sean, stay down." She didn't glance back at him, too focused on the men looking through the fence.

Sean hunched over, but kept his eyes locked forward.

Rome spun the wheel, crashing through the wooden fence. The men scattered, but the car clipped one of them, and another went beneath the grill screaming. Rome snatched the wheel in the other direction and the car lurched to the left, jumping the curb. The terrifying sound of metal scraping against metal overwhelmed the car as the Pontiac hit the road. Sean ping-ponged in the back seat. He regained his balance and looked through the rear window. They'd clipped the front of the black car the men had arrived in and torn the bumper off. One of their aggressors stood in the street, pointing and shouting and shrinking as Rome put distance between them.

———

They roared down American Legion Highway, skirting the cemetery. Rome took hard turns, zig-zagging down residential streets. They whizzed by parked cars, far too close and too fast. Sean marveled that they hadn't taken any side mirrors off. It was a miracle that no one stepped in front of the chugging vehicle, but Sean remembered the number one rule of playing in the street: someone always looked out and they cleared the streets when a car came.

"I got a full tank of gas and people I know in Philadelphia."

"No," Sojourner said.

"We'll cut through to 95, around the square, and avoid Blue Hill Ave as long as possible."

"*No.*"

"What? What are you talking about, Soj?"

Sean felt a surge of emotion, hearing the nickname only Rome and his father used for his mother.

"Mom, where's Dad?"

Rome muttered curses as he drove, focusing on the road.

"They came to our home," Sojourner said. "Over a dozen white men came. Your father was already there, we were getting ready to leave."

The heavy car thundered along, rocking as Rome navigated the neighborhood streets.

"They came. Shouting. Ordering your father to come

outside, claiming the authority of the FBI." Sojourner smiled. "Your father yelled out that their claim was 'bull-shit,' that they weren't any sort of law enforcement. I think he was really talking to our neighbors. People came outside, on their porches. The men weren't sure what to do. They had guns."

Sean's heart thundered out of control in his chest. It felt like his insides sloshed and moved of their own voli-tion. He cradled his torso, trying to will the vertiginous feeling to pass.

"Your father had so much integrity and courage. He was a brave man."

Was, Sean thought, remembering the incident down-town, how his father had fought and protected him. The relief when they were reunited.

"Dollar—of all people—you remember Dollar, our next-door neighbor?"

Sean nodded, a numbness creeping through his skin. Rome stole furtive glances at Sojourner, dividing his focus between the road and listening.

"Dollar—one of the worst people I know—came outside shirtless. He was wearing platform shoes and bellbottom jeans, this giant buckle of a lion's head. He fired a pistol at the bastards. One of them went down and Dollar stood defiant, a joint dangling from his lips. That's when they killed him. Gunfire everywhere, bullets shattered windows and bodies. I don't know who else on our street had a gun, but they fired back."

"Jesus Christ," Rome whispered.

"You came after that, Rome. David rushed ahead, but I didn't stop him. I should've told him, I should've showed him what I could do, long ago, and I never did. I've hid all this time. They shot him."

Rome made a breathless sound and said, "I saw you

through the back fence, holding someone. When you came to the car—the blood on your hands, I thought…"

"I couldn't get to him in time."

Rome made to turn left and cross Blue Hill Avenue, but Sojourner reached out and turned the wheel to the right.

Rome struggled with the wheel, unable to loosen Sojourner's grip.

"You killed that dude with your bare hands." Rome peered at Sojourner from the corner of his eyes.

Sean couldn't comprehend what was happening or what had happened. He'd barely wrapped his head around what his father had told him about his mother. Watching her hold Rome at bay like this was another helping of unbelievably he couldn't choke down.

"What the hell, Soj?" Rome made one last tug on the wheel.

"Into the Blue Hills."

"Why? God damn it, what the hell for?

"We have to go. It's time."

"Fine. We're on the road, let go of the damn wheel. We can hit 95 that way too." Rome shook his head and focused on the two-lane, winding road. "Shit, woman, what are you made of? Strong as shit."

Sojourner laughed, a high-pitched bark that sounded like agony to Sean's ears. His mother glanced at Rome, stifling a sad smile, and looked back at Sean, tears in her eyes. "Oh, my prince, it's too soon for this." She turned forward again, dropped her chin to her chest and covered her mouth.

Sean watched her shoulders heave as she stifled screams and tears alike. He reached forward and held his mother's shoulder. She was incredibly warm and placed one of her hands on his. Sean could feel something like wind moving beneath her skin, a gentle ripple. He'd imagined a marine creature might feel like this, mostly muscle held together on a skeleton of cartilage, if at all.

Nothing but the ache for his father made sense. A flood of everything pushed at his eyes, his ears, his nose, everywhere. With his father's death, it felt as if a gigantic portion of his head were missing. The pain overwhelmed him and he threatened to shut down, simply curl up and die in the back seat. But he couldn't, not with his mother still here. And he needed her. Sean needed her to stitch him up and hold him together, to show him that life without his father was still life and something worth doing. Because he didn't believe it, he didn't have the experience to understand any of this. He twisted in the seat, wracked with sobs and an indescribable pain that contorted his body.

A car with a missing bumper rounded the curve behind them.

Part Eleven: Back Again

Sojourner sniffed and said, "Into the first parking lot. We'll get out there."

Rome struggled with that for a moment and said, "What? There's nowhere to go there! What are y—"

"We'll go down the beach. It's open space."

"Open space? How does that help, Soj?"

"This way of unlife has gone on long enough. The monarchy is gone, that way of life is dead. I never wanted it, never needed the supporters. They never talked with me; they talked over me. A dying breed. I never should have stayed when they sent me. I should've gone right back." Sojourner looked into the back seat at her son. "But then I wouldn't have you." And her face split in sorrow.

Rome sputtered.

Sean slumped in his seat, his guts churning. It felt like his skin was going to slide off, but not before the top of his head exploded. He ground his teeth and pressed both palms to his eyes. His hands felt like putty, everything felt like putty and nothing smelled right. He tore his hands away from his face, tears leaving silvery streaks on his hands. From his position, he could glimpse the passenger-side mirror.

"Mom," Sean said. "Uncle Rome."

Rome was demanding answers and his mother continued to give unsatisfying responses while fiddling with her necklace.

"Mom, Rome! They followed us."

Rome glanced in his mirrors. "Shit."

Sojourner turned her head nearly all the way around, a cold flat look on her face. A flexibility Sean had never seen her display. Her eyes sparkled, tiny flecks of gold danced across the whites of her eyes and disappeared in her lashes. Sean couldn't trust his eyes. Everything was flowing with color in space, coursing liquid trapped in shapes.

"Soj, load this." Rome handed a pistol over.

She looked at it, weighing the weapon in her hand. Rome followed up with the bullets. She expertly popped the cylinder open and dropped cartridges into the chambers.

"Hurry, Rome. Turn into the lot at the pond." Sojourner handed the pistol back to Rome. He tucked it at his side.

"We can't stop!"

Sojourner put her hand on the wheel again.

"Soj, c'mon, don't do that again."

She stared at Rome, her hand gripping the wheel, long enough for it to be uncomfortable. She said, "We've known each other my entire life here. Please, Rome, you have to trust me. *Please.* For Sean's sake, at least."

"I *am* thinking of Sean! If we stop, they're on us."

"If David were here, you'd listen to him."

Rome glanced at Sojourner. Sean gripped the back

of the seat, waiting for what, he didn't know. They hurtled past the state police barracks near the park.

Sojourner said, "There isn't much time left."

"Okay, okay. Hold tight."

The parking lot near the pond had two entrances, wide openings in a chest-high stone wall with trees in front of it. Rome took them through the first on a diagonal, at speed. The car's wheels screeched, but they didn't slide. The right side of the car scraped against the stone, ripping off the side mirror. There were only a few cars in the lot, far away from the beach road. Probably hikers in the Blue Hills.

Their pursuers skidded to a halt just after the entrance, reversing to enter the lot.

Rome sped across the asphalt, aiming for the slim service road next to a playground Sean had spent many hours on while growing up. The metal seesaw that had scraped the skin off of his ankle was still there. He hated that thing and it was the last time he'd worn sandals anywhere.

The car lurched to a stop. The wheels spun. Sandy soil prevented them from going any further.

"I can't drive through this. What now?"

"On to the beach. Sean, let's go." Sojourner tried to open her door and it held fast.

The black car came flying across the lot.

Rome shouted, "Get out, go, go! Hurry!"

Sojourner put her shoulder into it and the metal creaked and popped open. She flipped the seat forward so Sean could climb out. Rome came around the car, the pistol in his hands. In the distance, they could hear sirens. Sean saw the flashing lights through the trees on the other side of the lot. The men in the black car hesitated.

The driver of the vehicle looked back and said, "Fuck them! We are here by the authority of the FBI, justice for America. Get those Commie niggers!"

"You ain't FBI, motherfuckers," Rome shouted. He turned and said, "I don't know what you got planned here, Soj, but I hope it works 'cause I'm out of ideas. I think this is as far as I go." Rome's lips were pressed tight and tears rimmed his eyes. "I've had enough." He nodded and muttered it again, to himself.

Sean's laid-back uncle looked more stressed than he had ever seen. Rome looked at him and said, "Your father was my brother, Sean, and your mother my sister. None of this matters without that. You hear me? It has to matter. I *love* you."

Sean nodded, unable to speak and not knowing what to say, regardless. He felt empty, devoid of anything, and hoping more than anything to stop the ache of losing loved ones.

Sojourner's voice hitched when she said, "Goodbye, Rome. Thank you."

Rome raised a fist to Sean and spoke through his tears. "Stay strong, young blood."

Sojourner took Sean's hand.

The police shouted at everyone to lay down their arms.

Rome grabbed Sojourner's wrist and pulled both her and Sean down behind the car.

The white men who'd instigated all of this shouted back, a cacophony of reasons and excuses. Their apparent leader, the driver, shouted them down and addressed the police. He was thin, wearing an ill-fitting suit, and balding with a thick mustache.

"Listen, we are here under the authority—"

"Get your hands up!" State police shouted from behind their cars.

The man, holding a pistol, stepped away from the car, his hands raised. "Listen! This is the Federal Bureau of Investigation's jurisdiction. These people are communist traitors and—"

Rome cut in. "Are you serious? You dickheads are COINTELPRO dupes?"

"*Assets*," the leader snarled.

Rome snorted and sucked his teeth.

One of the state officers shouted, "Badges! Real slow."

The leader of their pursuers pulled out a billfold and held it up. The police looked at each other, incredulous, before one of them said, "That is not an FBI ID. Get down on the ground. Now."

"Officers," the man continued, "that man is a member of the Black Defense Program, a known communist sympathizer, and a traitor. He and the people you're letting get away are—"

"Ain't you heard man? COINTELPRO is done! What the fuck do you think you're doing?" Rome stood up from behind his vehicle. "You out here killin' people over some shit that Congress done shut down?"

The police reiterated their commands. Only Rome and the white man were in their line of sight. The man spun and pointed with his weapon, "Shut up, nigger, that's enou—"

Rome shot him in the chest.

Everyone else opened fire.

Sean could hear police shouting over the gunfire. Everyone was screaming as he ran with his mother. He couldn't make sense of anything, his mind churned like his guts. The way his mother pushed him along made him feel like paper in a stiff wind. Bullets whizzed around them like hypersonic bees. Sean realized his mother was shielding him from the gunfire just as he heard the sickening sound of a bullet striking flesh.

Sojourner stumbled as another bullet hit her in the back. She cried out and directed Sean toward the lifeguard station and bathrooms. They vaulted up the steps. Sean hazarded a look back as his mother snatched open the door to the bathrooms.

In the road behind them, Rome lay sprawled on his back and the men who'd pursued them were gunned down in a desperate rush of gunfire. The state police were shouting at each other, trying to determine what to do next. One of them pointed at the lifeguard station.

"Move, Sean!"

Sojourner slammed the door and twisted the latch to set the bolt, locking them in. Sean peered around and confirmed they were in the ladies' room, nary a urinal in sight. For him, it was an unnatural place to be.

His mother swayed, taking deep breaths. Her skin shimmered with a sheen of sweat and something else. At that moment, the dingy, muted colors of a state-run building swam with the bright promise of more. In the quiet of the concrete room, his senses flowed with precision again and he was starting to see his mother as simpatico with that. It made him wonder what he was truly capable of.

"Mom, are you okay?" He reached for her.

She held one hand up and said, "Give me a minute, Sean. I need… a moment." Sojourner held the jewel of her necklace and leaned against the wall. She dropped her head and slid down to sit. Behind her, she left a vivid streak of blood.

Desperation overwhelmed Sean. He stood in place and shook, unable to move his mouth or his feet. He trembled and choked back a keening sound building at the back of his throat. His head throbbed and his heart pounded, threatening to tear loose from his ribcage.

Sojourner looked at her son and had to call his name three times before he focused on her. "That won't do," she said. "Keep an eye out the window. Tell me what they're doing."

Sean nodded vigorously and moved to the window. He could see the police moving towards them, crouched and guns at the ready. Through clenched teeth he said, "The cops are coming, Mom."

"Okay," she said and grunted.

Sean looked at her. He could see a faint glow between her fingers where she held the stone. She didn't move but her back did. It flexed in and out and twisted, then rippled and tightened. A metallic clatter on the concrete floor was followed by another. His mother had expelled the bullets.

Sean, breathless, his mouth hanging open, said, "I can't believe you can do that."

Sojourner looked at him and inhaled deeply. She straightened and said, "You can too. And more, maybe, I don't know." She shook her head sadly, "I should have told you sooner, should have taught you. I just… thought it was too early to worry about."

Sean's mind reeled. The incident with Donna. What he'd seen with her and with Lluvia. How he'd managed to hide from his father downtown. The way his senses went wild like they were peeling apart reality itself.

Sean said, "What am I then?"

Sojourner shook her head slowly and said, "New. Like me, more or less, but I grew you, Sean, *I built you* with your father's help and..." She swallowed hard and covered her mouth, physically holding back a wave of remorse.

My Dad, he thought as his stomach lurched. Sean clutched his head.

Sojourner sidled up to her son and hugged him from the side as she looked out the window. Reinforcements had arrived and the state police now formed a perimeter. One of them raised a bullhorn to his lips.

"This is the Massachusetts State Police! Come out of there now or we will remove you!"

Sojourner pushed one of the tilting panes open and shouted, "Stay back, I'm with the Black Defense Program and I have a bomb!"

"Mom!" Sean was aghast. "Why would you say that?"

"It will give them something else to think about rather than kicking in the door and shooting us."

"They wouldn't do that. Would they?"

"Sean," Sojourner took her son's shoulders between her strong hands. "The police in this country find it's easier to kill Black people than protect them."

Sean's body trembled again, he felt woozy and he couldn't stop crying. "What are we going to do?"

Sojourner straightened, her hands loose at her sides again. She sighed. "We wait."

"For what?"

"The transverse slide."

"The what?"

"You heard me, my prince." Sojourner crossed the room and sat against the wall. She flexed her neck and shoulders, skin rippling. "You need to be ready."

"I don't underst—"

"Sit. Here, across from me."

Sean stepped over and sunk to the ground, cross-legged. He was grateful the floor was dry. He didn't want to think too hard about what might be on the floor of the ladies' bathroom.

"This," Sojourner waved a hand at Sean, "is what you are right now. It's not *all* of who you are."

Sean stared at his mother. His mouth hung slightly open. She seemed shaky and spent, her skin still glowed with sweat and other things.

"I'm not explaining this well."

"No." Sean shook his head. "It sounds like you're saying I'm not… human."

"You are, my prince." She put one hand on his cheek. "And you're not."

"I'm…"

"Many things, everything. A biological adept, a mimic."

"That doesn't make any sense, Mom!" Sean sobbed into his palms. "You—different species can't—"

"I can't easily explain the biology, Sean, you are a product of your mother and father, just like any child. I'm not a scientist, I don't—"

Sean took a long shaky breath and said, "We're going to die, aren't we?"

Part Twelve: The Final Chapter

Sojourner looked at her son, peered at his life, everything she knew he was and everything he didn't know. She hugged him, pulled him close, and whispered in his ear that everything would be okay. Outside, men with guns shouted into bullhorns. Despite her abilities, it wasn't clear she could help Sean. The signal had been sent but it was possible no one had received it. Everything could have changed since she left. Despite her race's loose relationship with time, not enough of it may have passed or perhaps too much. She was still young by her own people's standards and the confidence she felt physically on Earth did not translate when it came to her own society. Bringing some comfort wasn't all she could do, however. There was the matter of preparing him for whatever may come. If they were to stay here, he'd have to survive whatever came next. If they were to leave, he had to survive that journey. The goal was clear, but the means were not.

Sean sobbed on her shoulder and the men outside

droned on. She relaxed and held him, trying to think, to formulate a plan. He pulled away and surged to his feet.

"Sean—"

He screamed at the window, "Leave us alone!" His voice cracked and trembled, becoming an involuntary screech. He thrust his hands out like claws with nothing to snare. He rode the anger until his perception slid and his grip on physicality became a fluid thing. The world around him took on an unearthly hue, emanating what he could only imagine was the full spectrum of reality. He could see and hear and taste everything and it made his head hurt, his entire self trembled. Something pushed at him, crawling from somewhere inside his body that he could only imagine was his soul. It was both familiar because of the last several weeks and it terrified him in its alienness. It was uncontrollable. He snapped back to reality when Sojourner pulled him away from the windows. She felt the tension in his skin, the way his muscles slid, and knew what needed to be done, but not how to do it.

"Sean, stop, listen to me!"

Her son wiggled and pushed, keen to get away and do something. She held him tight, still stronger than he was willing to be. She cupped the back of his head and forced him to face her.

"What do you want?"

"I want to leave, I hate this, I hate it here! Nothing is right! I'm never going to see my friends again."

She shook him and said, "Is that all?"

"Is that all?" He wailed. "Why won't you help me? Why did you let Dad die?"

That last hurt her, but she held on, and pushed. "Are you done?"

Sean clenched his teeth and writhed in her grip. "Leave me alone! Let me go!"

"No."

"You lied to me, you've lied to me your whole life! Nothing is real, I hate this, I hate it all."

"Is that it? You hate me? Is that what you think?"

He shook and bowed his head, unsure what to say or do while trapped in his mother's iron grip.

Sojourner shouted, "Is that it, Sean? Look at me! You hate me for living my life? For deciding how *I survive* day-to-day?"

Sean shook his head and struggled, mewling in his throat. He said, "I don't know."

She grabbed his chin and lifted his head. "I am your *mother* and if you listen to me, *we* will survive this. That is all you damn well need to know right now. You hear me, Son?"

Sean blinked a few times and nodded against Sojourner's grip.

"Good. Now don't say anything and just listen."

"Okay, but—"

"Shut it! Listen."

"Mom—"

"Just listen."

Sean, confused, focused on her and said, "To what?"

"To them, to me, to anything, but just stop. And listen. Hold your breath. Stop."

Sean blinked and she could see the thoughts churning behind his sparkling eyes. He was ready, so close but still so far out of touch with his own body. "Close your eyes," she said, "And stop doing. Just listen, don't breathe, let that go."

He nodded and closed his eyes before taking a deep breath. Then another. After one more, he held. The bullhorn blazed outside, nearly indecipherable. Nearby, a pipe hissed and birds called. His mother had gone silent. He floated with his thoughts, his memories.

His father had revealed so much and so little at the same time. Sean's emotions surged, a ferocious pressure built and he realized it was a new feeling. A mix of anger and sadness. Loss. He focused on his father, remembering the sound of his voice, the advice he'd given over the years. When he opened his eyes, he took a deep breath and said, "I don't have to breathe."

"Not as much as you think. What else did you notice?"

"How quiet I could be."

She nodded.

"When Dad couldn't see me downtown—"

"You must've blended in, mimicked what was around you. I need you to remember how you felt. You need to embrace that feeling and control it. This body is yours in more ways than you know."

A new voice, clear and distinct, cut through the air. A voice that projected calm. "Sojourner?"

Sojourner continued, ignoring the call from outside, "You need to remember those moments, Sean, everything you felt that was different, like the world wasn't what you remembered."

"Ma'am, please? Can we talk? My name's Lieutenant Clark Rogers, I'm a representative of the State Police. We've identified Mr. Rome Coleman, an associate of yours. Your husband is David Lenun, I believe? Nobody wants any more violence today. Please, let's avoid any more tragedy. Can you talk to me? Let me know you and your son are all right?"

She looked outside to see the man speaking.

Rogers leaned over and consulted a notepad another trooper held and said, "Sean. His name is 'Sean,' correct? We want to be sure he's okay."

Sojourner sighed. She watched him, a man with thin blond hair holding a megaphone. Next to him, a burly state cop and other uniformed officers were crouched down behind their cars, weapons drawn. Members of the press stood scattered around them, a sparse crowd of gawkers, with more arriving. Other police moved down the service road and along the beach to surround the building.

"We're fine, stop pointing guns at us, they won't stop a bomb," Sojourner shouted.

"I'm afraid that's not how it works ma'am," Rogers replied. "We need some assurances. You're threatening the safety of your son and us, we take that very seriously. Your friends out here were involved in a shootout, we take that very seriously too. We need to communicate with each other right now."

Sean watched his mother bow her head and clench her fists. He'd never seen her like this, barely contained.

Sojourner looked at her son from the corner of her eyes and told him, "Keep trying! Don't stop."

"But, Mom—"

"Don't. Stop." To the police outside she said, "Talk? We were attacked! Those men believed they had the authority of the government behind them! They believed *you* would support them. Why? Why is that?"

Sean slumped against the concrete wall.

Rogers said, "I don't know, ma'am, there are other officers handling that aspect. For now, right here, we want a peaceful resolution. I know you and your family were harassed by those men. They're no longer involved.

I want you and your son to be able to mourn peacefully and return to your home."

"It was more than those men," Sojourner shouted. "More than a dozen attacked us at our home! Callin' themselves FBI."

"That was a lie, ma'am, they were… misguided. The rest of them will be dealt with, the rioting on your street will take some time to sort out. The point is, there's no need for us to have a conflict here. That's done with."

"It's never done with," she replied. "You displace, harass, and kill people who look like me at your whim. Why? To assuage your fragile nature? Are we not a part of this society too?" Sojourner could see Rogers' face scrunch and his shoulders slump. She knew this line of communication would be frustrating for him. The white people of America did not enjoy being shown the monster they'd created. They tended to think it better to ignore the whole affair. Their behavior and rhetoric demonstrated that truth. In the meantime, they'd get down to the business of acquiring and hoarding resources while grinding down any dissenting voices. Same as it ever was.

"I can't speak to that, ma'am, no one out here can. We're state police and our job is to uphold the law in Massachusetts."

"What laws have we broken? Or is running from a racist attack against a law I haven't heard of yet? How do I know you're not here to kill me, to hurt my Son?"

The frustration was evident on Rogers' face, she could see it, even at this distance. "Miss, you are occupying state property and threatening violence against the police. That's a crime right there. But it's one that we're willing to overlook, under the circumstances. Now, please, come on out of there and let's work this out face-to-face."

"Assurances, Lieutenant Rogers. What can you say or do to convince me that we're safe? How about you lower your guns and calm down?"

Through the cracked window, Sojourner could see two dark vans pulling up to the front of the police barricade. Before the lead vehicle stopped, a man in a dark uniform hopped out and strode over to Rogers. The new officer reached for the bullhorn and Rogers held it back. A tense exchange followed.

Without warning, the temperature in the room rose.

Sean sat inside his thoughts. The world around him faded away, pushed aside by a wash of color and light. He could smell the water in the toilets and the pond outside. The crackle of activity outside came to his senses like swirling red waves of ink in water. All of his progress washed aside and collapsed in a wave of grief. He slumped and sobbed.

"Sean?"

He could feel his mother nearby, the sound of her shoes on concrete as she came closer.

"Dad's gone. Everything is going away, nothing's going to be the same again. I want Dad back, I want everything back the way it was."

"I'm sorry, my prince, but we don't have much ti—"

"Don't call me that, you don't care!" Sean pushed away from his mother and curled into himself. "You don't even care that Dad's..." He couldn't finish the sentence.

Sojourner kneeled and examined her son. "You don't think I *care*? That David is dead? About you?"

The only answer Sean could manage was a sniff. There was an edge to his mother's voice, a tone he rarely heard, if ever. The events of the past few days were things he'd never seen and hoped to never see again.

"You," Sojourner spoke softly. She cleared her throat and shouted, "You are the only thing left on this planet that I give a damn about!"

His mother's strong hands on his shoulders made him look up.

"I came here to hide. My arrival was… chaotic. And your father, in the midst of everything that was happening, reached out to me. He reached out and he helped. Without question. He was kind and thoughtful and willing to do the hard work to make this country a better place. And I loved him like no other for it. All I could do was learn to hate it here. The way this government treated people who look like us. Where I come from, my people—your people—are more direct. What is said is what is meant. Monarchy cannot last in such a system without devolving. Here, everything is oblique, a charade. It's impossible to know who's sincere or what their agenda might be. 'This is wrong' is a refrain that constantly runs through my mind. Your father wasn't like that at all and he knew better than me. To me, he was a beacon in all of this and I loved him.

"Don't you dare, don't you ever dare to say that I didn't care about your father. You hear me? I will knock what little sense you have in your head right onto the street, if those words cross your lips again. Do you understand me?"

Sean looked into his mother's face. Her eyes brimmed with moisture and her skin rippled, humming with emotion. It seemed like she was struggling to hold herself in place. Sean stopped resisting and flowed into her arms. They held each other and rocked. He realized his mother was humming to him; her entire body resonated with sound. It felt familiar and strange.

Outside, a new distorted voice came from the megaphone.

"You in there, listen up! This is Captain Maclaren with the State Police. I don't give a damn who you are or what your business is. If you don't come out of there with your hands where we can see them, we will be forced to remove you. You're trespassing on state property and you've threatened officers in the line of duty. We know about your involvement with the Black Defense Program. This is your last warning!"

The way the cop sneered 'Black Defense Program' and snarled his warning made Sojourner sigh. She gently removed Sean from her arms and said, "That is what I'm talking about." She crossed the room and looked through the window. Armed men were swarming around Mclaren, moving into position by the lifeguard station.

To Sean, it seemed as if his mother was about to say something to the people outside. Instead, she turned to Sean and said, "This is the end of our lives here."

"Are we going to die?" Sean trembled and struggled to control himself.

"Not by their hands, no." She removed her necklace and placed it on the ground in the center of the room. Then she stepped on it with her heel, applying weight until it cracked. She picked up what was inside and motioned for Sean to join her.

He refused, surging to his feet and turning his back. Sean brought his hands to his head and squeezed until he felt enough pressure to stop and open his eyes. He cast about the room, ignoring the melancholy pouring from his mother. Outside, he could see the police scrambling around the building at a safe distance. Men in black took up positions of cover facing the façade of the structure. Men in heavily armored uniforms assembled a pole of some sort.

"This is insane," he said, "nothing makes sense."

"No," Sojourner answered, "not much ever does here. But we make sense, my prince."

Incredulous, Sean spread his arms and slouched. The sound of his hands dropping to his sides was sharp in the room.

Sean asked, "Why can't we go home?"

"Because they'll kill us before allowing the story to be any more complicated than it already is."

"That's insane," Sean said.

"Yes." Sojourner straightened, watching her son.

Outside, the men assembling the pole finished their task. Another policeman lined up a shot with a squat, wide-barreled weapon. A tap on his helmet gave him permission to fire. The round punched through the window and pinged off the wall with a rattling sound. Acrid smoke filled the room.

Sean watched the sparkling emerald cloud billow across the floor to fill the room. He breathed in the chemical mess and blinked through the crystalline aerosol.

"I can feel it, taste it. I know it's supposed to sting, but…"

"Yes," Sojourner answered. "You're making progress. It's time. Come here."

Sean closed the distance slowly. From outside, the sound of boots crunching dirt and whispered, intense commands filled the air.

Sojourner showed her son the tiny device in her palm. The concave center pulsed with light. She wrapped one arm around her son's shoulders and said, "Push it."

"I'm afraid."

"Me too."

Sean pressed the center of the device and the room disappeared into sound and light.

Sean couldn't breathe. He was blind and burning.

I'm dying, he thought, *but I don't need to breathe.*

I don't need to see with eyes.

I don't need to burn.

The light enveloped him and he tumbled. Feeling stretched and beyond control, he clenched and felt an overwhelming pain. Every nerve screamed and he struggled to think, to remember what his mother had told him.

Remember.

Embrace it.

He was afraid, excited. Then and now. Instead of pulling back from it, he dove in, trusting his mother's guidance and how he felt when he tapped into his anger and sorrow. The tumbling stopped and he slid forward, like a dart extending along a barrel.

I'm more, he thought and extended further, *I'm more than the Black boy they see in America.* He let go and the swirling light carried him forward.

BLACK DEFENSE PROGRAM DETONATES BOMB AT HOUGHTON'S POND

In an apparent suicide bombing, Sojourner Lenun detonated an explosive device within the lifeguard station at Houghton's Pond in the Milton neighborhood of Blue Hills. Her son, Sean Lenun, was with her at the time. The incident followed a race riot in the Mattapan neighborhood of Dorchester involving her husband, David Lenun.

Mr. Lenun was a founding member of the black nationalist group known as the Black Defense Program, a militant black separatist group akin to the Black Panther Party. Mr. Lenun has also been on the FBI's radar for several years following investigations into the subversive activities of the radical organization. The violent conflict on the street occurred with citizens concerned about Mr. Lenun's ongoing activities with the BDP. Other aggressors, known collaborators and radicals, participated in the melee, leading to the death of Mr. Lenun and several bystanders. One of the armed BDP members on the street fired upon and murdered a concerned citizen, forcing the men to defend themselves. The men fought for their lives using whatever means were at hand.

Another associate of Mr. Lenun, and highly-ranked member of the BDP, Jerome Coleman, fled the scene with Mrs. Lenun and her son. Concerned citizens followed the outlaws to Houghton's Pond and alerted the State Police stationed nearby.

Police confronted Mr. Coleman in the parking lot. He was killed after firing upon the police. Mrs. Lenun barricaded herself in the lifeguard station with the bomb and her son. Despite several good-faith attempts by both State Police hostage negotiator, Lt. Clark Rogers, and tactical unit leader, Lt. Donald Maclaren, to get Mrs. Lenun to surrender peacefully, she detonated the device, killing several policemen and devastating the building. Mrs. Lenun and her son are presumed killed in the explosion. Their bodies were not found and presumed destroyed.

Acknowledgments

First and foremost, hat's off to Christopher Golden and Bracken MacLeod for harassing me into writing a semi-autobiographical coming of age story. To Paul Tremblay for making the fine point that not liking a thing means you should write the thing you like. To all the people whose heads turn like a confused puppy when I describe this story. To Leza Cantoral and Christoph Paul for recognizing stories that make people turn their heads like confused puppies need love too. And to my family who were made to look very weird in this story, I hope they don't mind, they inspired art.

About the Author

Born and raised in Boston, Massachusetts, Errick Nunnally served one tour in the Marine Corps before deciding art school was the safer pursuit. He graduated from the Massachusetts College of Art with the MCA Alumni Association Memorial Award and has been working in the graphic design industry for over twenty years. A published author, he enjoys writing, reading, cooking, art, and comics.

Also by CLASH Books

HER NEW EYES

T.J. Martinson

BEYOND THE PLANET OF THE VAMPIRES

Ulrich Baer

CATHERINE THE GHOST

Kathe Koja

THE MAN WHO SAW SECONDS

Alexander Boldizar

THE BLACK TREE ATOP THE HILL

Karla Yvette

WHAT ARE YOU?

Lindsay Lerman

VHS

Chris Campanioni

BAD FOUNDATIONS

Brian Allen Carr

THE LONGEST SUMMER

Alexandrine Ogundimu

DARRYL

Jackie Ess